TRAIL OF THE PINTO TO OREGON

Books by J. Paul Loomis

SALTO, A HORSE OF THE CANADIAN MOUNTIES

HORSE OF THE DEEP SNOWS

TRAIL OF THE PINTO STALLION

TRAIL OF THE PINTO TO OREGON

Trail
of the Pinto
to Oregon

J. PAUL LOOMIS

 DODD, MEAD & COMPANY

NEW YORK

1957

Library of Congress Catalog Card Number: 57-5417

Printed in the United States of America
by The Cornwall Press, Inc., Cornwall, N. Y.

To Dawn

Fiction is often the most effective way to tell the truth, for we remember best that which we have felt. So, in *Trail of the Pinto to Oregon*, I have tried to tell in a way that can be felt a story of the fur traders and mountain men in the days when trails across the northwest were dim—a story of the Indians of that region when they had been little changed from their original way of life.

A better writer could have woven a web of fancy that fits perfectly upon the framework of facts. As it is, the fiction at some points warps the frame.

I tell, for instance, of a visit of Captain Bonneville, the explorer, and our fictional Nat Kane, to the great trading fort on the Columbia where the city of Vancouver, Washington, now stands. Though Bonneville made two trips from the Rocky Mountains to the Columbia region he did not, on either one, actually visit Fort Vancouver. He did not, at the time of this story, meet the western manager of the Hudson's Bay Company, the patriarchal Dr. John McLaughlin.

This story is erratic in time only. Years later, when the region then called Oregon, but which is now the states of

Author's Foreword

Oregon, Washington and part of Idaho, had been established as United States territory, a military fort was built beside the trading fort of Vancouver—still the Pacific headquarters of the Hudson's Bay Company. The commander of the military post was our same *Colonel* Bonneville.

Another mismatching of time is that I placed in this story the Nez Perce boy Thunder-rolling-to-higher-mountaintops, who as a man became famous under the name of Chief Joseph. It is probable that Captain Bonneville was entertained by Chief Tu-eka-kas, father of Joseph. But the time of the captain's visit was five years before Joseph was born.

Yet I have followed the essential truth, as nearly as I can learn it, which is the truth of how the people—Indian, part-Indian and white—lived, thought and did in the time and place I have described.

J. PAUL LOOMIS
Santa Barbara, California

Contents

CHAPTER 1

Attack

Nat Kane tingled to the soles of his moccasins. This was the first time that Captain Bonneville and the men of his exploring party had entrusted Nat with the duty of night guard. The self-reliant youngster had been through many stern experiences during the past summer, here in the Indian country; but after all, he was only fourteen—or about that. He didn't know exactly. Uncertainty of his own age was one of the least of the troubles Nat had experienced as an orphan on the frontier.

But like any lively boy, Nat was eager to shoulder a man's responsibilities. And assignment to guard duty was certain proof that he was now rated a capable member of this group of men. Besides the captain, there were Tarno, Laramie and Brent. These three were Rocky Mountain trappers—"mountain men." With them also was the Crow Indian boy, Far Eagle.

Captain Bonneville was on a two years' leave from the Seventh United States Infantry. He was strict, but kind.

He had been most helpful to Nat and the boy's gratitude was deep.

Tarno was a stolid, stocky man of bearlike strength. Indians invariably called him Square-jaw. But he was contemptuous of all Indians, friendly or hostile. "Varmits," he called them, "a little smarter than catamounts!" Since Nat believed Indians to be people as real as any with white skins, he found it hard to like Tarno. But they had been comrades through difficult and dangerous times—through "hard doin's," as the mountain men said.

Laramie was a lithe, dark French Canadian with some Ojibway blood. He was as carefree as a hawk wheeling above a sunny plain—and much less stern. Nat liked Laramie. But Brent Logan was the friend Nat had known almost as long as he could remember. Brent was tall, tough, quick. He was a horseman to his heels. Brent could hit a bean with his Hawken rifle as far away as most men could hit a bucket. Brent had been like an understanding older brother to Nat, and it was to find Brent that Nat had made his way west.

He had crossed the plains as an orderly to Captain Bonneville in his trading, trapping and exploring expedition in this year of 1832. And having found Brent at last, Nat was superbly happy. And he was proud, now that they had permitted him to stand night guard.

It did not strike Nat as queer to say "stand guard"— when he did it on his stomach. Nat had never seen a military sentry pacing his post. But he knew very well that he must keep vigilant. This was dangerous country, for hundreds of miles in any way you went.

ATTACK

It was the region of mountains and high plains where the Missouri, the Colorado and the Columbia rivers all have a major portion of their source. It was country where the Crows and Blackfeet, the Shoshonies, Sioux, Gros Ventres and Arickaras all fought heartily among themselves. But they were now beginning to consider these early white men as intruders in a land they believed the Great Spirit had given strictly to them. To *stand*, literally, while on guard might enable lurking eyes, accustomed to the darkness, to silhouette one's form against the night sky. This might result in a silent—and silencing—hand upon one's throat and a knife between the shoulder blades.

So Nat lay upon the ground in some low brush.

Behind him, in larger timber, was the camp. But the fire had been put out. Nat knew that his comrades had wrapped their long rifles with them in their buffalo robes.

Not far above the crouching black bulk of a mountain, Nat could see the Seven Persons, Blackfoot name for the Big Dipper. Those stars and a host of others, washed bright by the sharp night wind, dimly lit a meadow in front of the boy. On it he could see vaguely their twenty horses. The only one he could identify from where he lay was Brent's big stallion, Kiowa. The pinto's white splotches made that possible. Brent had traded six better than average horses for him, to a chief of the Kiowa Indians, while on a journey to the New Mexican town of Santa Fe. Nat could hear the horses cropping grass and the thumping of their hoofs as they moved about, restricted by their *parfleche*—rawhide—hobbles.

Nat could hear many other sounds. And he knew that

3

upon his ability to identify every one of them might depend his life and the lives of his companions. For instance, was that distant yipping and wailing the howl of an actual coyote? Or the voice of a scouting Indian signaling other members of his war party? Was that a real owl that hooted frequently? That splash in the nearby stream, above the steady chuckle of its riffles; was that made by a beaver plastering mud on his lodge against the coming winter? Or by a wading Indian who had stumbled on a stone beneath the water? And these tiny stirrings in the dry leaves and pine needles near him—were all of them made by woods mice and pack rats?

But most sharply of all, Nat watched and listened for any alarm among the horses. This was not only for a sudden rush of hoofbeats, for a sudden silence while they looked and sniffed and listened could also mean danger. They could smell Indians.

They could also smell bears, wolves, elk and other animals not often dangerous. Their actions had to be studied. But uppermost in Nat's mind was the knowledge that most Indian attacks began with an attempt to stampede the horses of their intended victims.

The young explorer was quite aware that here on the Portneuf River this tight-keyed watchfulness might seem unnecessary. Didn't Captain Bonneville have the permission of Chief Big Swan to explore and trade in the country of the Blackfeet? Hadn't he been given a pipe of carved red stone as a talisman? That was to prove to all Siksiki —the name by which the Blackfeet called themselves— that the captain and Brent Logan were among the very few white men whom Indians of this fierce tribe counted as their friends.

It was as a result of events that had taken place in the Teton Mountains only a few weeks ago that Captain Bonneville and this little party had been trapped in a canyon, along with Big Swan's entire village, by a huge war party of the Absaroka, or Crows. Though outnumbered two to one, they had joined forces in their desperation and defeated the raiders, even though the Crows were aided by certain renegade white men—deserters from Captain Bonneville's employ.

But Nat knew that *all* bands of the far-ranging Blackfeet might not yet know of the pledge of friendship given, and that war parties of other tribes frequently ventured into the country of the Blackfeet. For the warlike Siksiki had enemies on every side of them. Such raiders might be very glad of the chance to get the horses, rifles, trade goods— and scalps—of this small party of white men. Yet Indians of any tribe rarely attacked unless they knew they could surprise their opponents. So Nat appreciated that Captain Bonneville was right in insisting that the men he led keep constantly on the alert. This the boy was doing so intently that he felt no hint of drowsiness, though he had been in the saddle all the previous day.

Suddenly he realized a danger from a wholly unexpected quarter. One of the horses of the band he was watching came purposefully toward him. He recognized the shadowy but well proportioned shape as that of his own horse Pierre. The animal moved quite freely, for he was only "side-lined." That meant that one of his front feet was tied by a strap

5

nearly a yard long to his hind foot on the same side. This would keep Pierre from running but it was not nearly so hampering or uncomfortable as the usual hobble, which tied the two front legs of a horse closely together. Pierre had caught the scent of Nat and he was coming over to be friendly. He did not know that he would thus reveal the boy's hiding place—if there *should* be lurking enemies.

"Go 'way, Pierre! Go 'way!" Nat whispered. A dog might have understood. But "Go away" is a command not often given a horse. Even the reproof in Nat's tone did not check Pierre, who was an unruffled rascal—and the greatest horse in the world, his proud rider was always ready to declare—except, of course, Brent's tall, swift pinto, Kiowa.

Nat knew that he couldn't quietly move away as fast as Pierre could follow him. It looked as though he must take the risk of having the brown horse stand over him and nudge and nip him until the pest grew tired of his game.

And then the sharp squeak of a woods mouse came from some place very near Nat. It came without the pounce of an owl or the velvety swish of his wings. Nat started, then replied as exactly as he could repeat the sound, for it was the signal used between himself and Far Eagle, the Crow boy.

Pierre recognized the scent of Far Eagle and showed no fright as the Indian silently crept up to him. It took but an instant for Far Eagle to untie the side-line . . . and another for him to glue himself to the side of Pierre, one arm over the horse's neck, one moccasined heel hooked over his back. He changed the outline of the horse hardly at all. In a moment even Nat could not see him clinging there as he rode Pierre slowly away among the grazing horses. Some time later Nat heard the squeak of the mouse again, within three yards of him.

"How do you move so like a shadow?" Nat whispered his question in the Absaroka language. Far Eagle had taught it to him while he was a captive of the Crows for a part of the past summer—and while this friendship between the white boy and the son of Swift Bear, the Crow chief, was growing.

"You, Talks-with-horses, will soon learn to move like an Indian."

Far Eagle called Nat by the name the Crows had given him for the way he showed his love of horses. In a similar manner, Laramie had given Nat a name for his luck and the good fortune he brought Captain Bonneville's expedition. Because, as Laramie put it in the Indian way, Nat's "medicine was strong," the mountain men called him Big Medicine. Since the captain still called him Nat, it was a bit confusing to have three names among but five companions.

"Unless Indians move silently," Far Eagle continued in his soft whisper, "how do we approach within bow range of elk and antelope? How could we Absaroka enter a Siksiki camp and take their best horses—the ones that are tied before their lodge doors?"

"You shouldn't be out here," Nat reproved. "You might injure your lame ankle."

"I will not hurt my leg, going upon my belly."

"You think I can't stand guard alone!"

"Didn't I just save you from trouble, maybe, caused by your too friendly horse?" Far Eagle managed to express humor, even in his low whisper. "Talks-with-horses has twice saved me from *enemies*."

Nat knew he was referring to a series of events, recent and tragic. Chief Swift Bear had been killed, treacherously, by a white man. In the battle that followed, Far Eagle had been stunned by a glancing bullet. On Pierre, Nat had carried him to safety.

Later, Nat had escaped from the Crows and rejoined Captain Bonneville. Far Eagle, who up to that time had been called Runs Ahead because of his swiftness, had passed his tests to become a warrior and had received his present name. In the great battle in the Tetons the two friends had, unknowingly, fought on opposite sides. This time a rifle ball had broken the young Crow's ankle and killed his horse. Defiantly he had awaited death by the lances of the victorious Blackfeet, when chance or "strong medicine" had led Nat to him in time to claim Far Eagle as *his* prisoner.

So they were here together.

The broken ankle was the immediate reason why Far Eagle had not gone back to his own people. It was healing well under the skilful splinting and care of Captain Bonneville. He could ride without injuring it. But the captain warned the restless young Indian daily that he must not yet put weight upon it—and that he was by no means fit for a long journey alone to the Bighorn River in the Crow country. That journey was through mountains whose high passes might already be filled with snow and whose every mile was a risky one through the land of the Blackfeet.

Nat did not need the Indian boy's words of gratitude to know, now, that friendship also held Far Eagle here with him. He remembered well how Runs Ahead had championed the young white prisoner against the sharp jokes of the other Crow boys. How patiently he had taught Nat Indian skills, particularly strength and accuracy with a bow. But Nat wondered now, as he often did, just how willingly Far Eagle was remaining in this company. Captain Bonneville's determination, the young Crow knew, was to reach the River of the West, the Columbia, and to follow it a great distance. It would be many moons before he returned to the Rocky Mountains. Was the hold of Far Eagle's friendship for Nat greater than the pull of his own country?

Indians, Nat had learned, loved to wander—but usually within the broad limits of a region they called home. They did not have the thirst to see what was beyond *every* skyline, such as had grown in Nat out of his rootless childhood and his association with Brent Logan and Captain Bonneville. He had heard Far Eagle repeat, earnestly and often, the words the white boy had first heard from Swift Bear, in the Crow chief's tepee. "There is no country like the land of the Absaroka. The Great Spirit placed the Crow country in exactly the right place."

But Nat let none of these memories and speculations dull his alertness as the two friends lay on guard, watching, listening. The breath of autumn in high country chilled the night air. Often the sonorous honking of southbound

Canada geese drifted down to them, sharpening Nat's urge to travel. Swift wings of ducks whiffed through the darkness and sometimes the night was rippled by the gabble of low-flying brant. Once, far up in the hills, a cougar screamed.

Nat judged by the position of the Seven Persons that it was midnight and nearly time to call Brent for the second watch. Mist had raised from the stream and hung in the hollows where the air was coldest. Out of one of these blurs of mist two objects moved. Nat thought they must be horses that had strayed without his notice. Far Eagle touched him.

"Elk," he said. And after a pause, "Maybe."

The shapes drew nearer. Any doubt that they were bull elk now left Nat, for he could distinguish the racks of their antlers. They moved in among the horses.

"I didn't know they'd do that!" he whispered.

Far Eagle's reply was an abrupt, "Stay here." Bow in hand, he wriggled forward.

"But we don't need food! We killed a buffalo yesterday," Nat protested. Far Eagle did not stop.

As soon as the young Crow was gone, a strange uneasiness came over Nat. It was made up of distress that an elk might be killed wastefully and of regretful surprise that Far Eagle would do it—plus his fear that his friend might injure his ankle. But deepening all these concerns was the strangeness of the idea that two bull elk would graze among the horses. Clutching his rifle, he crawled forward.

Nat had lost sight of Far Eagle. As he moved among the horses, he startled one of them, a buckskin pack horse.

The freedom of its movement in turn startled him. Certainly it could not jump that way if hobbles were upon its legs. And Nat remembered hobbling that horse at sundown. Had the strap come off because he had tied it so poorly?

Nat crawled toward the white splotches of Kiowa, looming in the darkness. He saw one of the elk close to the pinto. The lordly carriage of its antlered head had drooped and its legs were mysteriously shortened. Its body was almost on the ground beside Kiowa, while the big pinto was pulling away suspiciously. Suddenly the horse was free to go. The elk rose. It had but two legs!

And *then* Nat understood. The elk was a cleverly carried head and skin. It hid an Indian who was cutting the hobbles on the horses!

Nat's heart thumped so hard he feared the Indian might hear it. His hands were not steady as he thrust his rifle forward. He had fought, creditably they said, in the battle in the Tetons. But to shoot into a charge of Indians thundering down upon him, with men on either side of him fighting fiercely also—that was very different from crouching alone in the dark and shooting an unsuspecting person —no matter how certain he was that his target was an enemy. He cocked his rifle.

Nat had been taught by Brent that there is a way to do this silently; by holding the trigger until the hammer has been drawn back as far as it will go, then gently releasing the trigger into its notch in the hammer. But now the boy did not think of this until he almost jumped at the click the hammer made.

The Indian *did* jump—toward Nat! Nat's rifle roared,

rolling echoes through the dark hills the young guard didn't have time to hear. His bullet hit the elkskin, but not that portion of it behind which was located a vital part of the Indian. Pitching off the clumsy concealment, the Indian sprang at Nat, knife raised.

The boy was trying to get his legs under him and his empty rifle, long and heavy, lifted to 'fend off the descending knife. He knew he wasn't being quick enough, knew, too, that if he succeeded in saving himself from the first blow, he wasn't as strong or skilled as the Indian in hand-to-hand fighting.

He was sure that his shot had brought Captain Bonneville and the mountain men out of their robes with ready rifles. But they wouldn't be in time to help. The knife was coming down.

Zing . . . thud! The sounds were of a twanging bow string and a deep-driven arrow. There was a gurgling gasp. The attacking Indian fell on Nat . . . but limply. The knife dropped from his grasp.

With a violent shudder, the boy pushed the body from him and leaped to his feet.

"Down!" hissed Far Eagle, not five steps away. "*Ai-ee!* Your shot will bring their attack."

He was right. They could hear the sudden drum of hoofs. Nat wanted to reload his rifle. He wanted to get out of the path of the raiders and into the shelter of the timber. But even above these instincts of self-preservation, he remembered that Far Eagle *must not* re-break his ankle —and limp clumsily and humiliatingly the rest of his life. He wanted to carry Far Eagle, who was crawling as fast as he could. Then he thought of Pierre and sounded a short, three-note whistle that was his call for his horse.

The hoofs of the Indians' horses were thudding nearer. The rifles of Nat's friends in the camp were cracking in the dark. The air was snapping with excitement and danger. Would Pierre hear? Would he come? Nat repeated the whistle sharply.

And there in the darkness Pierre was beside him.

Nat boosted Far Eagle to the back of the brown horse. But even as he crouched to spring up behind his friend, he threw one more look around him.

Some of their horses, freed by the disguised Indians, were galloping past him. Some were plunging awkwardly along in their hobbles. Nat knew Kiowa was free. Was he leading the stampede? Then quite near, the white patches of the pinto stallion loomed in the dark. Head high, he was facing the onrushing danger.

Nat ran to him. He caught Kiowa's mane and, still clinging to his long rifle, scrambled to the pinto's back. He set Kiowa racing toward camp.

Arrows swished past him. Yells rang out. There was a banging of "fusees." That was the name the mountain men had given the inaccurate smoothbore trade guns that many of the Indians had obtained in Canada, where they were known by the French name *fusil*. Nat lay close to the running stallion's back and his chief dread was that he might feel the shudder of a bullet or arrow breaking the smooth gait of Kiowa. But unhit they reached the timber.

"Nat?" called a familiar, sharply anxious voice in the deeper darkness.

13

"Yes." The boy vaulted to the ground. "Oh, Brent, did Far Eagle get here?"

"Yep. An' your little brown hoss. Wagh, you two done *suthin'*, to save Pierre an' Kiowa!"

"But Brent—the rest of our horses! They're gone! What'll we do?"

"We aren't afoot yet, by a long ways. An' this scrap ain't over. Now you scoot over there with the cap'n."

Brent's long form leaped easily to the back of Kiowa. Lying low, he raced out across the dark meadow. Nat was wrenched by anxiety for Brent—one man against who knew how many? He could only watch the blur of Kiowa disappear.

But as the sound of the big pinto's hoofs blended into that of the Indian horses he was following, a second horse leaped out of the brush near Nat. It, too, followed the fading sounds of the Indian horses. And this second horse could only be Nat's own Pierre! *Who* had taken him, without so much as telling Nat he was going to? The boy groped his way through brush and trees until he found Captain Bonneville.

"Nat! My, but I'm glad to know you're safe!" The captain expressed his relief in a tense whisper. He stood behind a pine, reloading his rifle. He pressed the boy against the trunk of another tree.

"Who took Pierre?" Nat asked him.

"I don't know," the captain admitted in an exasperated tone. "Of all men that walk, mountain men have the least idea of discipline! I suppose it was Laramie. Tarno is less

14

likely to act first and think afterwards. *I* didn't order it. Nor did I order Logan to leave our camp, either."

Another drumming of hoofs swept toward them in the darkness. Just to their right, a rifle cracked. That should be Tarno. The captain, seeing that Nat had reloaded his rifle, also fired at the sound of the hoofbeats. But he had observed a rule followed by all bands of men fighting with muzzle loading rifles—never to empty all weapons at once.

Arrows and bullets aimed at the gun flashes, snipped through the brush or thudded into tree trunks around them. Nat, in his turn, also fired at a fusee flash. The pounding of hoofs veered away.

"This war party," muttered the captain, "must be a fairly large one, to be attacking our camp at the same time they are stampeding our horses."

"And Brent is out there among them!" Nat breathed, unheard. "And Laramie!"

Then a low hiss announced and identified the approach of the rifleman on Nat's right. A shadow took shape among the surrounding shadows.

"Where's Big Medicine? Did de boy get to camp?" The whisper had a distinctly French-Canadian accent.

"Laramie!" Nat exclaimed. He was immediately clapped on the shoulder with rough affection.

"Thank *le bon Dieu!*" murmured Laramie.

"We thought it was you who rode away on Nat's horse," exclaimed Captain Bonneville.

"*Non.* Laramie likes his hair where it is—not on an Injun's belt," was the answer.

"But I *didn't* suppose it was Tarno!"

15

The surprise still in the captain's tone was echoed anxiously in the thoughts of Nat. The anxiety was not only for the rider but for Pierre, as well. Tarno was rough with horses.

But, Nat thought, Tarno would say the rough part was on the men—to be *without* horses. He had doubtless seen what he believed was a chance to help Brent recover their lost herd. Tarno was cautious by habit but fearless when need be. There had been no time to hunt up Nat in the darkness and ask for the use of Pierre. Tarno hadn't even asked the captain's permission to go after the stolen horses; for that matter, neither had Brent. No wonder Captain Bonneville, used to leading soldiers who acted only under orders, had his troubles leading mountain men. *They* thought of waiting for orders about as often as did the eagles who wheeled above their hills.

The captain, Nat and Laramie, spaced along the edge of the timber, waited in readiness. But the attack did not sweep back. After the two bursts of shots, yells and the thudding of hoofs, all the usual night sounds were choked. The mountains, woods and meadows around them seemed holding their breath. The minutes stretched into time enough for a man to walk a mile—for a horse to run five of them. Then, far away, a shot echoed and re-echoed. Two more shots confused and multiplied the echoes and one more shot prolonged them unbelievably. But at last they rolled away to silence.

Nat fidgeted anxiously. Many times he looked around him, straining his eyes as well as ears. By and by, Laramie approached him, silently.

"Too many mice around," he warned.

"It was me," Nat explained, "calling Far Eagle."

"Humph! I hain't seen him, neither. *H'sst!*"

There was a faint throb of hoofs, growing in the distance. Laramie glided back to his post. The sound of many horses came steadily nearer. Nat steeled himself in readiness for another attack.

He was afraid, of course. They were but three defenders. But the anxious waiting had stretched his nerves to such brittleness that action, even in surging danger, promised relief. When he could see a shadowy band of horses pouring into the meadow, he raised his rifle. But a call rang clear.

"*Hi—ya-a-ah!* Don't shoot thisaway. It's me, Logan. Bringin' in most of our hosses."

That voice rolled a lot of the anxiety off Nat. He could see the moving blob of white which he knew was Kiowa and tell by the way Brent was riding the pinto that neither of them was hurt. He couldn't yet see anything of Tarno, with Pierre. Nor did he know what had become of Far Eagle. But it was good to feel they again had enough horses to get them out of this danger spot and continue their journey.

As the horses loped across the meadow, they shied suddenly and the herd split. But it came together again after the horses had passed the thing that had frightened them. Nat knew what it was—the body of the Indian who had worn the elk skin. The horses reached the camp and stopped against the timber, blowing and snorting. Most of them were tired enough to permit themselves to be

17

caught easily, but a few were still so excited by the stampede that they had to be roped. Nat and Laramie tied the animals behind the camp, in the middle of the clump of timber. Laramie was delighted to find that *his* horse had been returned safely.

Nat, too, admired the fast, strangely marked horse that was the pride of Laramie. It was a dark red bay, with a light roan rump, deeply spotted. Laramie had explained to Nat that, since horses so marked were originally found only among the herds of the Paloos Indians, a small tribe on the plains of eastern Oregon, such horses were called Paloos also. They were rare and were highly prized by any Indians who could trade for them or steal them.

Before they had finished tying the horses, another hail came from the dark meadow.

"Wagh!" It was the mountain man's all-purpose exclamation, in the sandy voice of Tarno. He took shape rapidly, dropped to the ground and, without one glance at the horse he had been riding, strode up to them. "Guess we're off'n our ankles agin. Never did like walkin'," he said.

"Where *you* been?" Brent demanded.

"With ye," answered Tarno, in a tone that bristled slightly. "With ye, as nearly as that turtle of a hoss could keep me. I got a poke or two at the Injuns when ye druv 'em off the hosses. I been ridin' rear guard for ye all the way back. I see we got one of the red cusses, anyhow, out there on the meadow," he finished callously.

"H'm!" was all of Brent's comment.

Nat had run to Pierre. He found that the heaving

flanks of the brown horse were dripping. He got his *apishamore*—a saddle blanket made from the skin of a buffalo calf. With this he rubbed Pierre, then led him slowly back and forth. Neither Kiowa nor any other of the horses in the herd showed such hard effects of the run. Nat's blood boiled. But along with Pierre, he gradually cooled down.

He'd been in the mountains long enough to know there were times when Indians and mountain men alike spared neither horses nor themselves. But if this were one of the times when such riding was necessary, Tarno might at least have shown concern for the horse when the ride was done!

"Come to bed," Brent said to him. "Laramie's on watch. You an' the rest of us need what sleep we kin get 'tween now an' mornin'."

Even after he had tied Pierre, however, the troubled Nat crept through the dark timber around the camp. Softly yet anxiously he called. But he found nothing of his friend, Far Eagle.

CHAPTER 2

Grizzly

At dawn they saw an Indian on the meadow. He was crawling toward them. Instantly Tarno's rifle was trained on him, while Laramie's came to a ready. But this time Nat's eyes were keener than those of the mountain men.

"Don't shoot!" he cried. "It's Far Eagle. And he's hurt. Can't you see that?"

Nat would have galloped out to his friend Pierre but Brent put a firmly restraining hand on his shoulder.

"Mebbe it's a Injun trick," he said. "Right now, at the edge o' daylight, is the time to expect more mischief. Mebbe the Injuns nabbed the youngster last night an' are using him to decoy us into the open."

"Wagh!" agreed Tarno. "Last night I heerd the Crow war whoop. An' that youngun's a Crow, remember. This hoss will bet he went over to the Injuns on his own account."

Nat stiffened in surprise. He had not thought of their

20

attackers being a party of the far-ranging Absaroka. Since they were in Blackfoot country, he had presumed them to be Blackfeet who, unaware of the promise given by Big Swan—or in defiance of it—had made the attack. But Far Eagle would instantly have recognized the war cry. How he must have been torn between two loyalties! It would have been natural and right, Nat thought, for the Crow boy to go over to the men of his tribe. But Nat's fists clenched at Tarno's sneer that Far Eagle would now attempt to betray his white friends.

That resentment filled the boy for the moment. And with it, concern for the further injury Far Eagle might have received. It was not until the young Indian was near and Nat could see that his face was marked, not by physical pain but by grief, that the white boy realized its cause.

To save Nat, Far Eagle had driven an arrow through the Indian in the elk skin. And it was *then* that they had heard the yells of the attack—the Crow war cry, which Nat, but for his desperate effort to find Pierre and save Far Eagle, might also have recognized. *Then* the Indian boy had known he had killed one of his own people!

That was why Nat could not find him. For after the Crow warriors had swept by, Far Eagle must have crawled back to the meadow in the wild hope that the Indian he had shot was not dead—that perhaps he could save him. Nat met Far Eagle at the outmost fringe of the timber.

"Did you know him?" he asked. Far Eagle blinked once in surprise that Nat understood so much.

"He is Two Antelopes," the young Crow replied. And after a pause: "He was my father's friend. I have often

21

listened to his stories in our lodge. Many times he went with my father to fight the Blackfeet or the Sioux. After the battle in the Tetons—if I had gone home then to the Absaroka, I would not have killed him."

"But you were crippled! And if you had started home alone, you would have starved or been frozen by now, in the high mountain passes; or been killed or captured by the Blackfeet. And I would have been killed by Two Antelopes. At least, that's what we suppose." Then he questioned, with a depth beyond his years, "Who knows, ever, *what* might have happened if we'd done differently? I know you cannot help it that, as your people say, your heart is on the ground. But it isn't right to blame yourself."

Far Eagle said nothing. But a little of the sadness seemed to have left his eyes.

Captain Bonneville and the three mountain men did not share Far Eagle's grief, as Nat did. To them it was a relief to know that the attacking Indians *were* Crows, for Crows on the Portneuf, they thought, would be only a band of marauders who had tried to use an unexpected opportunity to kill and rob a small party of white men. The attack did not mean, as was first feared, that the mighty tribe of the Siksiki had decided to reverse Big Swan's permission to Captain Bonneville to explore their land.

"Ask him," the captain said to Nat, with a nod toward Far Eagle, "how many Indians attacked us."

Nat interpreted and Far Eagle spread the fingers of both his hands, meaning ten. But he shrugged to indicate an uncertainty.

"Sounded like thirty," grunted Tarno.

"Ask him if they are gone," said the captain.

Far Eagle made no response. This might be to protect his tribesmen. More likely, Captain Bonneville was fair enough to realize, it was because he did not know, but believed he would be blamed if he gave an answer that proved wrong. The captain did not demand a reply. He examined the young Indian's ankle, muttering his surprise that it had not been re-broken in the night's activities.

Brent and Laramie had already begun the usual but risky morning task of finding out whether it was safe to break camp. On fast horses, they were scouring the country for a mile on every side. They found no Indians. So the horse herd was turned loose again to graze, under the guard of Tarno and Captain Bonneville, who had breakfasted while Brent and Laramie rode.

Nat tried to cheer Far Eagle but there seemed nothing he could do or say to lift the young Crow from his dejection and self-reproach. The white boy had already learned that Indians, no matter how stolid they might appear in the presence of white men, were sensitive and emotional. They were deeply affected by triumph and happiness, or defeat and sorrow, as Far Eagle was now.

Soon after sunrise, the men saddled and packed the horses. Captain Bonneville, on the tall buckskin he called Cougar, led the cavalcade. Brent and Tarno ranged on either side as scouts and Laramie and the two boys, driving the pack horses, brought up the rear. All eyes were constantly alert as the pack train made its way on up the Portneuf River, into the higher hills.

"Big Medicine, you must see all dere is to see," said

Laramie, stressing the same theme that Brent, too, had often hammered home in instructing Nat. "See it, an' *know w'at it means*—eef you goin' live to be mountain man! W'at scare dose wild duck from de river? W'at muddy de water in dis crick? Who dat bluejay scoldin', bear or Injun? Dat moccasin track you find, is she made by friendly Shoshoni or by cut-your-throat Na-de-wi-sioux? Dat w'at my Ojibway people call 'em. Name mean rattlesnake. White men make it 'Sioux.' "

When they reached the rim of Old-man-on-his-back Plateau they rode up a slope nearly to the edge of the tableland. Brent dismounted and untied from his saddle the skin of a coyote. This he placed over his head and shoulders and crawled to a point where he could see over the plain. Indians, if there were any to see him, would have to be very near to distinguish him from a curious coyote peering between the rocks. After a survey, he returned to the group.

"Damp gunpowder an' no fire to dry it!" he exclaimed, meaning that something perplexing had arisen. "There's a line o' critters you can just make out for hosses, far yonderly. Could be the Crows who entertained us last night, though there 'pears to me to be more pack hosses than a Injun war party would have. Yit a band of Injuns with their squaws an' gear would raise a bigger column o' dust by their travois poles draggin' on the ground. Better each o' you have a look."

They did, still taking care to remain concealed, for the horsemen on the skyline might not be the only ones around. All Nat could see was a line of dots and a curl of dust.

24

"Injuns packin' home meat fr'm a hunt," Tarno said.

"Trappers," declared Laramie.

"What? White men going ahead of us into Blackfoot country! With no permission, such as we have!" Captain Bonneville spoke incredulously. "That's something no one has dared."

Laramie shrugged. "You de *bourgeois*—boss," he said.

"Oh, come!" The captain's tone was impatient. "Because I hire you doesn't mean I can see farther than you can; or even that I am as experienced as you in matters of this country. But I find it hard to believe that white men, other than ourselves with our safe-conduct talisman, would risk an expedition into this forbidden region."

"Cap'n," said Brent, "I don't say for sure that those *are* white men. But I do say that *any*thing could happen. The American Fur Comp'ny, with John Jacob Astor's money back of 'em, an' Fitzpatrick, Bridger an' Sublette's Rocky Mountain Fur Comp'ny are fightin' each other fang an' claw. Yes, an' the Hudson's Bay is sendin' trading brigades from Oregon. Any one of the three would twist the Old Nick's tail to get an extra beaver plew (pelt)—or to keep their competition from gettin' one. And," he added meaningly, "they all count you as competition, you know."

Nat and Far Eagle were the only ones that offered no opinions. The party returned to the dim Indian trail leading up the Portneuf River. Brent and the captain still had furrows in their brows.

On Nat the question of the caravan they had seen rested lightly. The crisp, thin air was sweet in his lungs. The sky was startlingly blue and the surrounding mountain tops

25

were vivid against it. The frosted cottonwoods along the river were gaudy gold against the sober green of pine and spruce. Here and there a red bush of kinnikinnick flamed.

They were now too high above the plains to see many antelope or buffalo but bands of elk and mule deer frequently crossed the valley ahead of them. On cliffs they began to see the grayish-white *ahsahta*—as the Crows called the bighorn sheep. Their flesh, Nat had heard the mountain men agree, was the finest meat in the world.

"Remember that old ram you shot with your bow last summer, while I lived in your tepee?" Nat asked Far Eagle. "And the big soup spoons you cut from his curved horns?"

Far Eagle's lips smiled briefly but his eyes remained clouded.

All the small streams they crossed were dammed into a succession of ponds, in each of which stood a domed beaver lodge. Laramie pointed to them in excitement.

"*Sacre!*" he cried. "Me, I could take forty prime plew here in ten days eef dey let me set my traps."

But Laramie and all the rest knew that Captain Bonneville had promised Big Swan that they would do no trapping while in the Blackfoot country. The Canadian could release his enthusiasm only by further instructing Nat.

"Dat *Castor*, de beaver, he's de smartest feller in fur," Laramie declared. "He know he's got to stay under de ice all winter 'cause his feet is bare an' dey freeze eef he put 'em in de snow. But he know how high to build his dam to make pond dat won't freeze to de bottom. He dig long canals so he can float de aspen he cut to his pond where he sink it wit' mud. Come winter, he's got room to swim under de ice an' lotsa bark to eat. Got warm lodge dat wolf can't break, 'cause *Castor* cover it wit' mud an' she freeze lak iron. He's smart to trap, too. Some old beaver nobody ketch. Good thing, else soon dey all be gone."

This was a jarring thought to Nat. It was natural for him to hate wasteful killing of game. But it had seemed impossible that the thousands of elk and millions of beaver and buffalo could ever be destroyed. It would not be by Indians alone, surely. They killed only what they needed. For themselves they took only enough beaver skins to keep them warm.

But now the white men had come. They brought an unlimited demand for pelts because, so Nat had heard, in some way as mysterious to him as to the Indians, from beaver fur magnificent high hats were made. In a place called Europe, which lay beyond an ocean and in the "eastern States," of which the boy's knowledge was also vague, every gentleman *must* have one or more of these hats. So for beaver pelts the traders would exchange guns and knives, blankets and beads and vermilion paint. And to get these things they suddenly needed—or thought they needed—so very much, the Indians now killed ten times their former number of beaver. Still, because they expected to continue living in the regions they considered theirs, they always left *some* animals to breed.

Not so the white trappers. They stripped a region and moved on. Nat recalled now, how, at last summer's rendezvous—the great gathering of traders and hunters—he had heard the trappers say of certain streams or ranges of hills: "Trapped out. Not enough fur thar now to patch yer shirt!"

And he remembered that on his way west, although he had seen hundreds of buffalo trails deeply worn into the prairies along the Kaw and Blue rivers, not one buffalo had Captain Bonneville's expedition sighted until they reached the valley of the Platte. It was an unhappy subject to think about—game and fur becoming scarce. Unlike the Indians of the rich bottom lands of the Kaw, who grew corn, the Indians of the plains and mountains depended upon game for nearly everything—for food, clothing, tepees, shields, storage panniers, tools, ornaments, cords, thread. And again, for food! Without game . . .

That picture was so dreary Nat's mind could hardly hold it, especially while the fascinating sight of game in such abundance was right before his eyes. He tried to use this interest to brighten the mood of Far Eagle, pointing out a sleek brown otter swimming and diving in the river, a squirrel peeking at them around a tree trunk or a black bear sitting drolly upon his haunches to watch them pass. With a nod or a word Far Eagle, in each case, let Nat know that he had seen the animal first. Then the fact of his keen watchfulness was proven, strikingly.

Brent Logan, still scouting for hostile Indians, was riding along the brushy side of the valley, a hundred yards above them. He was not on Kiowa but on a roan mare, because the pinto had been given a hard run during the night and another at daylight. Following Far Eagle's gaze, Nat saw a sunny patch of open ground. It was on the slope a little below Brent. Yet Brent could not see it clearly because

28

of a thicket of serviceberry bushes through which he was having difficulty in riding.

Then Nat started as a piercing shout broke from Far Eagle. The word was in Crow but warning was unmistakable in the tone. Nat's puzzled eyes saw only two tawny lumps in the open patch—bear cubs, asleep in the sun. *They* weren't dangerous!" What Nat failed to recognize was that the bears were *not* black bear cubs.

But Far Eagle's call had made Brent catch his rifle in both hands. Even that much preparation was vital, for he was able to swing the rifle and fire at a huge brown shape that rose, taller than his horse. It had lunged at him. Nat saw the smoke but the crack of the rifle was blurred in a throaty roar.

A dreaded realization clubbed Nat's mind: Grizzly! Unknowingly, Brent had ridden between a silvertip and her cubs.

Unless wounded, even these fearless monsters would rarely attack a man. But they did so surely and with an awful fury when they believed their cubs were threatened in any way.

The smash of the bullet heeled the bear momentarily off balance, for the downsweep of her great paw missed Brent. It broke the neck of his mare. She dropped like a wet sack. Nat saw his friend go down with the horse. But he knew Brent had kicked free of his stirrups, for, instead of being trapped under the mare, he sprang to his feet. With his knife only, he faced the standing bear.

Horror seemed nearly to strangle Nat as he saw Brent hooked into the bear's thick, crushing arms.

29

Captain Bonneville, Laramie and Far Eagle were spurring their horses up the slope. Nat realized he, too, was riding toward the grizzly as fast as Pierre could carry him. Only glimpses could be seen of what was happening in the brush and, though the men raised their rifles repeatedly, they could not risk a shot at the bear for the danger of hitting the man.

"Brent!" Nat cried in a voice he scarcely knew as his own. "Brent!"

Yet before they reached the fight—it was over. The huge bear sagged to the ground, releasing Brent as she fell. He straightened, staggered, recovered his balance. His long belt knife was red with blood.

Brent gasped through open mouth to renew the breath pressed from his lungs. One tough sleeve of his buckskin shirt was ripped to ribbons and the arm it had covered bled from shoulder to wrist. His powder flask, made from the horn of a buffalo, had been crushed in the furious jaws. That much the bear had done after the bullet—as they found later—had passed through its heart. Brent's knife had cut the aorta, the great artery, before the grizzly fell.

Her half-grown cubs had disappeared.

"They been weaned long time," said Laramie. "Ole lady kick 'em out to shift for demselves 'fore she hole up for winter sleep. But till she do, she fight for 'em lak *Diable*. Eh, Brent? You mighty lucky it don't cost you more'n a ripped arm to have right to wear necklace of grizzly claws!"

"I reckon you're right," Brent admitted when he had recovered breath enough to speak.

GRIZZLY

Captain Bonneville got out his small kit of surgical instruments. While Brent set his jaws against the pain, the captain stitched up his gashes with deer sinew. Tarno, meanwhile, retold the story of Hugh Glass; though all of them but Far Eagle had heard it by many campfires.

Hugh had been so badly torn by a grizzly that his companions were certain he could only live a few hours. Thinking themselves in great danger of Indian attack, they had left Hugh, unconscious, to die alone. Only he didn't. Living on berries, snakes, the flesh of a buffalo calf killed by wolves, Glass had crawled through enemy Indian country to Fort Kiowa, on the upper Missouri—a distance of more than a hundred miles!

"An' he's still huntin' buff'lo for the fur forts," finished Tarno, "tougher than dried bull meat." Tarno was incorrect, though he'd had no chance to know it. Nor did Nat learn until the next summer's rendezvous that the scarred old Glass had at last "gone under," killed by Arickaras at Fort Union.

This brought out other classic tales of the endurance of mountain men. Of Kit Carson who, after standing off Comanches all day from behind the bodies of his dead mules, had jogtrotted seventy-five miles during the night for a drink of water. And of John Colter, captured by Blackfeet and turned loose naked by their chief for the sport of watching his young men run the white man down.

Barefoot on the stones and cactus, Colter had run for six miles and outdistanced all the Indians but one. Turning suddenly, he had gripped and broken the Indian's spear and killed him with it. Then, bleeding, sweating, gasping; he

31

had dived into the Yellowstone River and come up under a heap of driftwood that floated against the point of an island. There he had remained in the icy water until dark, while the searching Indians sometimes walked directly over him. With only the blanket of the Indian he had killed and the broken spear, he had walked three hundred miles in seven days to Manuel Lisa's fort—to re-equip himself for another trapping expedition into Indian country.

"An' dat man," expostulated Laramie against the whimsy of Fate, "died in bed on a Missouri farm! But no wonder—drinkin' de brew of dead catfish in low-country rivers after he'd grown used to de cold, sweet water of mountain streams!"

All this was recounted while Nat's admiring eyes watched the deft fingers of Captain Bonneville. The captain was not a surgeon but his success at removing bullets and arrows and setting broken bones had done much to maintain the health of his own expedition and to relieve suffering among friendly Indians he met. But Brent surveyed his wounds ruefully.

"This game arm, Cap'n," he remarked, "won't be much help to you in case of another Injun attack."

"We'll try to avoid that," the captain said.

Nat knew he spoke the truth—which was no reflection on the courage of Captain Bonneville. That courage had been proven, all the way from Fort Osage on the Missouri, particularly in the battle in the Tetons. But Nat respected his friend and leader just as much for the fact that, army officer though he was, he would rather prevent a fight than win one—and that by fair dealing toward the Indians and by constant alertness, he *had* many times kept trouble from getting a start.

Now, because his forehead was moist from the concentration of his efforts, the captain removed his black army hat. The baldness of his head, in contrast to his black beard and the shoulder-length hair of the mountain men, was an unfailing surprise to Nat and a marvel to Far Eagle. All Indians who had seen this wonder called Captain Bonneville, in their various languages, the Chief-who-has-been-scalped.

Once more the party took up the trail and by early afternoon they reached the headwaters of the Portneuf. They crossed a ridge that divided it from the watershed of Roubideaux's River; named, like so many streams in these lonely mountains, for a trapper who had ventured there and been killed by the determined Blackfeet. It was from the valley of Roubideaux's River that the unknown cavalcade they had seen in the distance had undoubtedly climbed. But it had come from some place far down the stream.

This valley was steeper than that of the Portneuf and for a long ways there was no beaver sign. The voice of the swifter stream was more harsh. The chill in the air seemed to Nat to be more than just the afternoon shadows. Were he an Indian, he thought, he would believe his "medicine" was warning him. A raven flew over, uttering his guttural "*Quoke . . . quoke!*"

The men rode silently, even more watchfully. Brent checked them with upraised hand at the bank of the first beaver pond. Before Nat knew why they had been stopped he saw sudden anger glint in Far Eagle's eyes.

33

"Well, I'll be stomped by buff'lo!" Tarno ejaculated.

"Smashed!" exclaimed Laramie, his dark brows drawing down much like Far Eagle's. "Somebody's smashed de beaver lodge."

"No Indian would have done that!" broke from Captain Bonneville.

His declaration was also an admission that Laramie was right in saying that the party that had been in this valley ahead of them was composed of white men. The captain's tone hardened as he asked, "What object could anyone have for destroying a beaver house—when it's too late in the year for the beaver, if any are left, to rebuild it!"

"You're right about Injuns, Cap'n," Brent said. "They wouldn't an' didn't do it. If proof's needed, here's the flat-footed tracks of a white man on the crick bank. In some way, those trappers ahead of us have learned that we are follerin' them."

"Could have larned fr'm the Crows that pitched into us last night," put in Tarno. "They'd be all grins an' hand-shakes to a bigger outfit o' whites, which they knew they couldn't lick."

"Anyhow," Brent continued to Captain Bonneville, "white trappers couldn't imagine us having any other reason to be here than the same one that brought them— to get the most beaver the quickest way possible. So what they can't ketch, they'll destroy rather than let us take it."

Captain Bonneville shook his head drearily and re-mounted Cougar, his buckskin horse. They rode on down Roubideaux's River. At every pond the story was the same.

The beaver lodge had been demolished, its few remaining inmates frightened away.

"Some of de homeless beaver may crowd in wit' other, more lucky, ones, if dey find any, down-river," Laramie told Nat. "But most of 'em will be tryin' to build new dams an' lodges we'en freeze-up come, snap! It shut *Castor* out of de water. Wolves an' *loup-cervier*—w'at you call cougars—make a nice meal of Castor, then."

That thought now darkened the afternoon for Nat more heavily than did the mountain shadows. Then he heard Brent saying to Captain Bonneville:

"I wouldn't give a worn-out moccasin, now, for that red stone pipe the Blackfeet gave you as a safe-conduct talisman. Just let 'em ketch us on this river, where the beaver's not only been trapped but the last of 'em wasted, like this! *We* didn't do it—no. But how'll you say so to arrows an' fusee balls? War—an' no chance for words—is what we'll git from the Blackfeet, now."

CHAPTER 3

Blackfeet

When the explorers camped that night they did not risk a fire. The horses were not allowed to graze until after dark and then but for a short time, guarded by Tarno and Laramie. Captain Bonneville, Brent Logan, Nat and Far Eagle huddled behind a shelter of spruce boughs which they had raised against the night wind that sucked down the valley from the already snowy mountaintops. They had eaten their supper raw. For a long time they sat in silence with their thoughts.

"It galls me to sneak like this where we have a right to go openly," said the captain. "I'm mighty reluctant to give up my plans of exploring the Blackfoot country. But I'd rather drop them now than fight against my friends."

" 'Specially when it's sure to be a losing fight," Brent said. "When the Siksiki find us—an' be sure they'll track us if we stay here, no matter how we try to cover our trail— they'll fight all the more bitterly for believin' that we have,

36

as they put it, 'talked with two tongues.' They'll out-number us, while we aren't eg-zactly at our best."

"I know," the captain agreed. "The gashes that bear gave you have stiffened in the cold and make you feel pretty low. But I'm sure you're not speaking discouragingly just on that account. We will go back to Horse Prairie," he said decisively. "That is where the other bands of my men were to meet us after their fall trapping. I can surely find some of them in the region and leave word of my intention, which is to go on to the River of the West and Oregon—now—without waiting until spring."

To Nat, the announcement was like a spur. The River of the West, the great Columbia! To be sure, each present day of what they were doing was to him brimful of excitement and satisfaction. Yet ever since he had accomplished his first purpose of finding Brent Logan, his dreams had raced on westward . . . on, through he didn't know how many ranges of mountains, to the clear and mighty river and the fertile country of great forests called Oregon. In the saddle and by campfire he had heard men tell of it ever since he took the trail with Captain Bonneville, 'way back at Fort Osage.

So now, when the captain said that, without further delay, they were going on to Oregon, Nat scarcely felt the sudden movement of Far Eagle, beside him. Later he remembered it when he was trying to understand his friend's deeper than usual silence. How could the captain's words have meant anything to Far Eagle, who knew no English?

Or did he? When Far Eagle was teaching Nat to speak

Absaroka, he had seemed to make no effort to learn Nat's language. But now he had been a month among white men. Nat felt certain that the alert young Crow had understood the captain's words regarding his change of plans, and that it affected the Indian boy very differently from the way it spurred him. This silenced Nat's desire to talk about the coming adventure, as the two boys rolled up in their buffalo robes for the night.

At daylight, the party saddled their horses to start back to the Portneuf River and Horse Prairie. Then Far Eagle extended his hand to Nat, white man fashion. Nat, puzzled and suddenly uneasy, did not take it.

"I am going back to my country," Far Eagle said quietly, "and to my people. I would like to go with you to the River of the West. But not now. Too far. I would be too long time getting back to the Absaroka country."

"But why must you return soon?" Nat's voice was sharper than he meant it. But night before last he had lost Far Eagle for a time and the hurt had taught him how much the young Indian meant to him. Now this was like a second cut in the same wound. "You can come with us to Oregon," he urged, "and go back to the Crow country next spring."

"No," Far Eagle replied. "Last night, while I slept, I saw my totem, the white-headed eagle, in the sky above me. It spoke of Two Antelopes, the Absaroka I killed. His children are hungry. Tall Elk, the brother of Two Antelopes, was killed in the fight in the Tetons. Now there is no one to hunt for the family. They will be more hungry before spring."

"But the other hunters of your tribe will not let them starve!" Nat protested. "They will be hungry for a much longer time if you are killed by Blackfeet and never return than if you are just delayed while you go with us to Oregon."

"Talks-with-horses has already spoken of the danger of the Blackfeet," said Far Eagle, "and of the deep snows. And I have listened. But now the white-headed eagle tells me to go home and kill meat for the children of Two Antelopes. I must obey my totem. His medicine will help me.

"Yet I could not go away in the night without saying this to you," Far Eagle continued. "Also, I have no horse of my own here. I cannot ask for a horse of Chief-who-has-been-scalped. He would say I must not go. He has been good to me. I do not want to steal one of his horses. May I take the bay you sometimes ride?"

"No."

Nat's voice was gruff and for a moment he would not trust it to go on for fear it might quiver unmanfully. "If you *must* go," he said then, "you will take Pierre. He is fast. He will not fall with you. I escaped from your Crow village on him. So if any horse can carry you through the Blackfoot country, Pierre can do it."

Only Far Eagle's quick intake of breath told Nat how the offer had moved him. Nat uncinched his saddle and lifted it from Pierre. But he left his *apishamore* on the horse. Far Eagle would need the extra robe on a winter trip through the Tetons. Nat placed over it Far Eagle's saddle of buckskin, padded with deer hair. Now his eyes were smarting and he looked downward as he gripped Far Eagle's hand. His other hand twisted its fingers in the mane of Pierre.

"My heart is on the ground," Nat said, dropping naturally into the Indian form of expression. "But I know that your heart will have swift feet, for you are going home. Next summer, I will come back and find you and Pierre. We will hunt buffalo again together."

"You *must* come," said Far Eagle, "for Pierre will always be your horse. This winter, when the snow is deep, I will cut much cottonwood bark for him to eat, to keep him strong."

They mounted then and followed Captain Bonneville and the rest of the party, back toward the Portneuf. Without turning, Nat knew for a time that Far Eagle and Pierre were on the trail behind him. Then, also without turning, he clearly knew they were there no longer. He heard no rattling stones or cracking brush, no distinctive sound of their going. But he was pretty sure it had required a slim, strong hand on the nostrils of Pierre to keep the brown horse from whinnying *his* good-by.

The four men of the party, watching sharply for lurking Blackfeet, did not miss Far Eagle for some time. Laramie was the first to demand, "Where's dat Crow young feller?"

Nat tried to appear surprised. "Far Eagle was there behind me the last time I looked back," he said truthfully. He reasoned that if time were spent hunting for Far Eagle *here*, the Indian would have a longer start.

"No use, Nat. You're a poor pretender," said Captain Bonneville. "If you just now missed both your friend and your horse, you'd be more excited than you are. When did the Indian leave our party?"

"I think it was about three miles back, sir. Honest, I didn't see him go."

"Which means he is more than six miles from us by now," the captain said. "He is very foolish. But it would be more foolish for us to try to overtake him now." He reined his horse back to the lead, saying over his shoulder, "I wish him luck, for your sake especially."

"Humph! He's a gone beaver," Tarno grunted. Laramie shrugged, but in his expressive way that was not a gesture of indifference. Brent alone lingered to put his hand for a moment on Nat's shoulder.

"You must have thought a lot of that Injun," Brent said, "to let him have your hoss." But none of them seemed to miss Far Eagle for his own sake, which increased the weight of loneliness on Nat. Besides, the day turned dull and the mountains around them grew dark, aloof and foreboding. By noon, a cold drizzle was falling. Buckskin, which all of them were wearing, makes the warmest of garments so long as it is dry. But wet, it is clammy and disagreeable. The mountain men endured their discomfort with set lips, as they had done a hundred times before.

"We're lucky if it don't turn to snow!"

Tarno's comment also expressed the feelings of Brent and Laramie. But Nat was a miserable figure, hunched on his bay horse, Whitefoot. He was wishing for camping time hours before it came.

This time they made a fire, for the need was so great it overpowered the risk. They lit it before dusk. "Smoke doesn't show far through the rain," Brent said. He added, "But the damp air will make it lie clost to the ground where an Injun can smell it fer a mile." The flame warmed and dried them, halfway at least. It seared their venison. Then they put out the fire as the gathering darkness made its light sharply visible.

The next day and the next they hurried on, with keyed watchfulness. Once they barely avoided meeting a file of mounted warriors. Again, just in time, they found they were approaching a hunting camp of six lodges—Blackfoot, they were certain, by the single smoke flap at the summit of the tepees. From then on, they abandoned the trail by the river and made their way along the sides of the ridges, keeping just below the crests. It was rougher, harder going. But to stay in the valley meant that their tracks would quickly be picked up by other travelers. Eventually the trail they had already made would be found, surely. Speed and caution were their only means to keep from fighting Blackfeet. And fighting any members of this tribe with whom they had recently exchanged pledges of friendship was a thing Captain Bonneville and Brent were determined to avoid.

Nat knew that Laramie more than agreed with them. Willing though he was to take most things as they came, Laramie was especially reluctant to fight Blackfeet because he was half Ojibway. And, as he had explained to Nat, the Ojibway were ancient enemies of the Sioux. Since the Blackfeet had fought the Sioux ever since the Ojibways had driven them out of the forests by the Great Lakes, westward onto the Plains, Laramie felt a kinship with the Black-feet through their common enemy.

But the attitude of the hard-jawed Tarno affected Nat differently. "Injuns are Injuns," Tarno said. "A Crow arrow, a Sioux knife, a Blackfoot bullet, one'll kill ye just as dead as t'other. Only way is to beat 'em with yer own galena." Galena, in the versatile dialect of the mountain men, meant bullets, because the lead from which each man moulded his own came from mines at Galena, Illinois.

But as they traveled, this party kept their own galena in their rifle barrels. Not once, for the sake of killing food, did they risk the noise of a shot. This did not mean that they starved. Nat, because of the teaching of Far Eagle, was a good shot with a bow. He carried, in addition to a rifle that belonged to Captain Bonneville, a bow that had been taken from an attacker of their camp in the Tetons. It was one of the short, powerful horn bows that were rare on the Plains and in the Rockies because they were made only by a few skilled bowmakers among the Nez Perces, who lived farther west.

Just as the Crows made the toughest bull-hide shields and, strange as it may seem, sometimes traded them to their enemies, so the Nez Perces occasionally parted with one of their horn bows. For such a bow a Blackfoot would gladly give a fast buffalo horse, or even a gun. There were times, too, when the Nez Perces lost a horn bow in battle. The one Nat carried had belonged to Antoine Laronde, a half-Sioux who had deserted from Captain Bonneville's expedition.

Soundlessly, with this bow, Nat killed a deer or an elk as often, now, as meat was needed by the party.

They camped where Old-man-on-his-back Plateau made an unbroken skyline behind them and the river wound away into a wide plain. "One more day," Captain Bonneville said cheeringly, "and we'll be out of the region the Blackfeet claim as their own."

He spoke too soon. That night, with shots, a drum of hoofs and the guttural *"Howgh-Owgh!"* of the Blackfoot warcry, wild riders ran off nearly all of the horses of the little band of white men.

Four of the horses they rode most often and which were picketed nearest to where they slept were all they saved. Though awed by the disaster, Nat gulped a breath of relief when he saw the white-splotched form of Kiowa among the mounts still with them.

"We'll not have the luck to get the herd back this time," Brent said, while Captain Bonneville and the others barricaded themselves with the packs of trade goods. "By the sound, there's at least thirty warriors. This hoss says we'd better run for it right now, 'fore the Injuns swing back an' ring us in."

"And leave goods that cost a thousand dollars in St. Louis —plus that much more to get them here?" Captain Bonneville exclaimed.

"Or leave our scalps," Brent said.

"Wagh!" Laramie agreed with him.

"But there are five of us—and only four horses!"

"Kiowa kin carry me an' Nat." Brent paused. "But it's you that gives the orders."

"We'll follow *you*," the captain said, with no further word about his losses. He took from his packs only his small case of surgical instruments and an extra horn of powder and pouch of caps and bullets. He threw his saddle on Cougar. Tarno's horse was among those lost. He took Nat's, and the roughness of his hasty hand on Whitefoot's bridle hurt Nat—even while he knew their situation was desperate. The boy scrambled to a seat behind Brent on the pinto stallion's back.

They rode away cautiously, keeping their horses at a walk to lessen the sound of their hoofs. It was a clear night. Although there was no moon, the stars gave more light than they wished. They skirted the few clumps of timber that were near, then had to lead out across open ground. Immediately they heard the distant thudding of hoofs.

They rode for it then. "Every man for himself!" the captain ordered tersely.

Yells rang out. Shots ripped the night. Neck or nothing, the fugitives raced over the rough ground in the dark. They trusted everything to their horses' eyes and sense and sureness of foot.

For a time they were a tight group; leaping gullies, crashing through and over sagebrush, sliding into and scrambling out of ravines. Then Laramie, lean and light of weight and mounted on his fast Paloos horse, pulled ahead into the darkness until Nat could no longer see the blur of the horse's light-colored rump. Next Tarno, heaviest man of the four and riding the lightest horse, began to fall behind. And then Captain Bonneville's buck-

45

skin went to his knees at the bottom of a gulch. Though Cougar recovered and scrambled out, some bruise or sprain that he had received slowed him after that. Soon Captain Bonneville also fell behind.

Contrary to the orders of every man shifting only for himself, Brent reined Kiowa around. He rode back toward the dimly seen but clearly heard line of Blackfeet. He swung behind Tarno and the captain and slanted off on a course to the left of their line of flight; across the front of the fanned-out pursuit. The red and white pinto was far more easily seen in the dark than the other two horses, as the increased yells of the Indians proved. The pursuers in the lead followed Brent. The rest followed the leaders. So far as Nat could tell by his glances backward, the entire chase had been drawn away from Tarno and Captain Bonneville.

How Nat wished for Pierre! If he were on Pierre, the load on Kiowa would be that much lighter. Yet it was a lot of comfort to be right where he was, clinging to Brent's waist. Also, he was willing to admit that, even double loaded, the pinto stallion might be faster than Pierre. And for Far Eagle's sake, Nat was glad that neither Pierre nor his Indian friend was here.

Nat was scared, certainly. No matter how great his confidence in Kiowa, he knew the Blackfeet were famous horsemen. Famous raiders, too, who took what they wanted from the other tribes, particularly the peace-loving Nez Perces who raised the best horses north of the Spanish herds in California. Behind Kiowa were many picked horses, being lashed by their riders in this reckless chase. And

Kiowa was carrying double! Nat was light but Brent was a tall man, lean and steel-hard.

Kiowa's hoofs pounded on, more heavily now . . . losing their rhythm. Their drumming was slurred as they more often scuffed the sod. It was less distinct as the stallion's breath came louder. But on they thudded . . . and on.

The many hoofbeats behind gradually grew fainter. The yells of the Blackfeet ceased. Brent and Nat and Kiowa were out of the broken, brushy ground now, alone on a wide plain.

"Horse Prairie," Brent said. He stopped Kiowa and he and Nat leaped to the ground.

"No other horse could have run away from 'em!" Nat exulted. He tore up handfuls of dry grass and fell to rubbing the pinto stallion's sweating shoulders, haunches and heaving flanks.

"Reckon not," Brent agreed, an unmistakable pride edging through the matter-of-factness of his tone.

"Have the Indians turned back?" Nat asked.

"Mebbe. They've made a good ketch as it is. Fifteen hosses an' all that loot! But more likely they've just slowed down to save their hosses. An' spread out more to make sure they don't miss us in the dark. Come daylight, they calculate to see us or to find our trail."

CHAPTER 4

Nez Perce

Nat and Brent went steadily on in the darkness. They walked most of the time, leading the pinto to allow him to regain his strength after his magnificent race.

"He may need it—an' then some," Brent warned.

They swung their course back to the direction in which they hoped to find the others of their party. The stars paled. The sky above the black bulk of the mountains grew silver. Around them, the darkness thinned. The sage near at hand, trees and buffalo in the distance and wraith-like antelope, became distinct. When the sky above the mountains was yellow, curtains of mauve and rose hung above the other horizons. These vanished when the shafts of the sun shot out from between the mountain peaks.

Brent and Nat found Captain Bonneville leading his limping Cougar; then Tarno, astride the sweaty White-foot. The bay's head hung so wearily Nat couldn't suppress a low, angry cry.

"Get off," the captain ordered Tarno.

48

"I *been* walkin'," Tarno defended himself. "Wore a hole big as a dollar in my moccasin!" Grumpily he got down.

While they were wondering what had become of Laramie, a rifle shot came to them, small but clear and sharp through the thin air. Brent frowned. His restless eyes had already picked out riders in the far distance, behind and on either side of them. Remounting, the four set off at a steady trot.

They saw the spotted-rumped horse and found Laramie calmly roasting antelope loin over a fire of dry sage. He shared it with them. When Brent remonstrated with him for firing his rifle, he gave his ready shrug.

"Reckon I don't tell de Blackfeet anything they don't know. So why go hongry? Want to carry some of dis meat?"

"Our horses are already overloaded," Brent said.

Laramie looked at the riders in the distance and at his clean-legged Paloos horse that grazed on the dry bunchgrass hidden under the sage. He decided to take a haunch of the meat.

The party rode on as rapidly as they could, Brent and Laramie impatiently holding their pace to that of Tarno and Captain Bonneville. The Indians, as yet, did not come nearer but Nat could plainly see that those on either side were pushing farther ahead. They would not attempt, as they had last night in the darkness, to ride the white men down. They knew that in daylight the whites would make a stand. Regardless of their great superiority in numbers, they had a sound respect for the accuracy of the trappers' rifles. Indians, unless furious or desperate, seldom made a charge in which it was certain that some of their number would be killed.

Nat knew that this was not because Indians were cowards. Most of them were intensely brave. But they fought as individuals, not as a group blindly under orders. Each man prized his own life highly and was deeply saddened by the death of a comrade. Each chief felt himself responsible for the lives of those he led. To them, caution was not cowardice. Nor was a warrior to be sneered at if he said that his medicine told him to go home instead of into a fight.

So the Blackfeet were now attempting to form a circle around the white men. Nat could picture how quickly they would narrow it to bow range. Around and around Captain Bonneville's little band would go the wild riders, each hidden on the far side of his horse, each shooting under his horse's neck with amazing strength and a fair degree of accuracy.

By their hideous yelling they hoped to strike fear into their enemy, weakening his aim and endurance. By the sheer number of bullets and arrows fired, they counted on enough hits to finally kill all of the besieged band, without much loss to themselves, other than powder and lead—and time, of which they had plenty. Even the arrows could be reclaimed.

This method of Indian attack in the open must have proved a good one against other Indians, for it was standard all across the Plains. The Indian nature is excitable, and easily depressed. Later, the method proved effective against inexperienced troops and against poorly organized immigrants. But it was not, as Nat knew from what he had already seen and heard, very successful against mountain men. A veteran soldier like Captain Bonneville and seasoned trappers like Brent, Laramie and Tarno, didn't get rattled, didn't scare, didn't give up. They used their packs as a barricade. They had better weapons and a more skilled and deliberate aim.

But this little band had no packs to lie behind. They were outnumbered five to one. And they had no water—in case they lived long enough to need it.

"If we can only reach the Snake River!" exclaimed Captain Bonneville.

"The Injuns an' their hosses kin swim it better'n we kin," growled Tarno.

"But there's a little shelter along its banks! And at least there's water!" said Captain Bonneville. "It isn't far, now."

"Yep," agreed Brent. "But at this rate, our chanct to git there 'fore the Blackfeet ring us in is as good as the chanct of a one-legged man to win a high-kicking contest!" His tone was matter of fact. Each person could see that the Indians were nearing steadily and that the lame horse, Cougar, and the overloaded Whitefoot were at the limits of their speed—painful limits that brought unashamed tears to Nat's eyes. He jerked on Brent's arm.

"Let *me* ride Whitefoot," he cried in a voice shrill with urgency. "Take Tarno in my place. Kiowa can carry even two *big* men faster than Whitefoot is going now."

For a long moment Brent made no reply. Was he weighing the idea? Or ignoring it? Then his hand reached

51

back to Nat's thigh—the part of the youngster he could most readily reach. Logan was an undemonstrative man. Nat was at the age when a boy is most reluctant to show or accept affection. But Brent's brief, hard grip gave Nat assurance and a marvelous feeling of how much his friend cared.

Then Brent reined Kiowa close to the horse of Laramie. The Paloos was loping with so little effort it was plain that Laramie could have left them, and the pursuing Blackfeet, easily. He had done so in the dark. But then there was no intention of making a stand, a fight. Now they would soon be forced to do so. Laramie whipped 'round from scanning the Blackfeet to face Brent. His black eyes glinted. His nostrils dilated. Relish of danger was keeping him here with the rest of them as much as loyalty to the group. Brent caught Laramie's rein and brought both the Paloos and Kiowa to a stop.

Laramie spilled out a jabber of questioning French.

"Take the captain with you on your horse," Brent said. His tone was one that *had* to be obeyed, for Brent knew, as Nat only sensed, that Laramie was used by lifetime habit to looking out for just himself.

"But can Nat keep up?" Captain Bonneville questioned anxiously.

"Nat kin ride," was all Brent said. By it he meant that Nat could do more than just stay on a horse.

The captain knew that the slowness of his lame horse was one of the things holding all of them back. He saw that Nat and Tarno had not waited for orders to exchange places. He scrambled up behind Laramie, regretfully leaving Cougar where he was.

More than once it had been necessary for Nat to ask of a horse all the speed and strength there was in him. He had asked it of Pierre when they were escaping from the Crows—of Kiowa when he had raced against Jim Bridger at last summer's rendezvous and the stakes were "winner takes the loser's horse." But never before had it been necessary for him to call for so much from a horse when there was so little strength left in him. Just an ordinary little horse, too, that Nat hadn't valued very much.

But Whitefoot responded, the very best he could. True, it was a relief to him to have the weight he carried reduced by nearly half. But more than that was the difference to Whitefoot in having a rider who sat like he was alive, not a bag of gravel—who *asked*, instead of demanded, his horse's strength. Nat put all his own strength and spirit into the race, along with Whitefoot's. Somehow the bay kept up with the others—in spite of his stumbling gait and whistling breath.

And there was the river, broad and silvery, before them. The Blackfeet, on either side of them, were lashing their horses to close in front of the little band of white men. But the Indians, Nat dared to believe now, weren't gaining fast enough to cut them off! They'd make their stand at the riverbank, where they could be attacked from one side only. Maybe they could even swim the river!

And then Nat's jaw dropped—and short, harsh words broke from the men, for over a ridge beyond the river rode a great wave of mounted Indians. They were yelling

53

and banging fusees. They swept down the slope toward the river like wind across the brown grass. Nat's heart seemed to be under the stumbling hoofs of his horse.

But he rode on toward this new overwhelming force because Brent and Laramie did so. And because one didn't just *quit*, even when there was no longer a chance!

The Indians beyond the river were opening and closing their ranks and swerving their swiftly running horses in well-drilled figures. Nat knew it meant something—but his numbed senses could only see in it a display of savage triumph. From Laramie, however, it brought a waving of his rifle and a joyful whoop.

"Sacre bleu! Les Nez Perce!" He looked back toward his comrades, his face split in an exultant grin. *"Les Nez Perce,"* he yelled again at the sight of their bewildered faces. "Friends!"

A burst of shots behind them made Nat look back. The Blackfeet were just getting into range. They had recognized the identifying maneuvers of the Indians beyond the river even more quickly than Laramie, knowing, as they must have, that there was no such sizable force of their own tribe over there. Now they had closed into a group and were shooting to vent their anger at the sudden change in the situation and in the hope to yet score a kill. Their bullets kicked up dust around the fugitives. But, fired from running horses at long range, none of them hit.

Laramie, in the lead, rode splashing into the river. When the water grew deep enough to cause his mount to swim, he threw himself off on one side so the horse would not sink so deeply and could swim faster. He clung to his reins and his saddle pommel with one hand and with the other held his rifle above his head. Captain Bonneville slid off the rump of the horse and gripped its tail. Brent waited at the water's edge for Nat to go ahead of him. There was good reason to doubt that Whitefoot could make it to the farther shore.

As he had seen Laramie do, Nat swung out of his saddle when his horse started swimming. Whether the cold water refreshed or only frightened the weary Whitefoot, he swam for the first few moments with startling strength, but with the stubbornness of terror. Since it was easiest to go with the current, he struck straight downstream. No matter how Nat pulled his head to one side, he would not turn.

Brent tried to put Kiowa below Whitefoot and force the bay toward the farther shore. But though on land the big pinto could carry two heavy men faster than the weary bay could carry Nat, swimming and towing those men through the water was something else. Burdened so, Kiowa could not even keep up with the frightened pony. And all the while the bullets of the Blackfeet splashed around them.

They were spent bullets, but still capable of killing if they hit a vital spot. And nothing much but the heads of the men and horses showed above water. The Blackfeet could now have overtaken their quarry, could have ridden to the river's edge and made sure of their aim, but they did not. The Nez Perces, whooping and riding up and down the farther shore, were firing at the Blackfeet.

The mighty Siksiki were jealous of their reputation as warriors. They were angry and chagrined at losing the white men whom they believed had destroyed their beaver.

But they were *not* going to plunge into a fight against double their number—not even of the Nez Perces, whom they ridiculed for preferring peace to war and for being friendly toward white men. Nevertheless, under the froth of their scorn, the Blackfeet knew that these men from beyond the Bitterroot Mountains were brave, skilled warriors, once they determined to fight.

Nat was still trying to turn his horse across the current, but Whitefoot was frightened past understanding. Once again, how much Nat wished for Pierre! That stalwart horse always kept his head—a head full of good sense! Yet even now Nat was glad Pierre was with Far Eagle.

The chill of this water that was straight from mountain snow fields was driving into the vitals of both Nat and Whitefoot. The horse was sinking lower as he swam. His rasping breath splashed the water in front of his distended nostrils. His eyes bulged. But he clung to his downstream course.

"Leave him!" yelled Brent. "Swim for it alone. I'll help you."

But Nat remembered—even if Brent seemed to have forgotten—how his friend's arm had been torn by the grizzly. It was a long ways from well. That would cut Brent's swimming strength. Nat had almost no confidence in his own ability, alone in the water, especially now, with the cold so nearly paralyzing him. Yet what really determined the thing the boy did was his refusal to abandon Whitefoot, to be swept on down-river until he drowned.

Nat pulled himself over the bay's back to the off side. In this case it was the more dangerous side because it was

toward the firing Blackfeet. He lost his rifle doing so.
But now, instead of pulling the head of his horse around
with his rein, Nat pushed on Whitefoot's jaw and neck.
He stroked it, too, and talked to the horse—though he
wondered how there could be any reassurance in the sounds
that came through his chattering teeth. Clinging to his
saddle with his left hand, Nat kept pushing with his right
against Whitefoot's neck. He put all his strength into it
—and all his feeling for the little bay who, though not as
smart or fast or strong as Pierre, was still doing the best
he knew.

Then, suddenly, Nat could see that the horse was swimming *across* the current. The far shore was *ahead* of them
—and a little nearer. But the current, still carrying him
down, made the shore sweep by him rapidly.

Then Nat saw one of the Nez Perces break from the
galloping throng and ride into the water toward him.
Bullets splashed on either side of the Indian, too. But on
he came. Soon his horse was swimming beside Whitefoot.
The rider, a moonfaced young fellow, was grinning assurance at Nat. Even though his face twitched once in startled
pain, the grin came back.

He gripped Nat's rein. His strong, fresh horse helped
—almost towed—the exhausted little bay.

Then the feet of both horses struck bottom. In a moment a dozen Indians were pulling Nat and Whitefoot up
the riverbank. Over his shoulder, Nat saw other Indians
helping Brent and Tarno and Kiowa.

Nat was swung to the back of a horse, behind one of the
Nez Perces. The whole band rode swiftly to the summit

of the ridge over which they had first come into view. Here, out of range of the Blackfeet, they dismounted. Even the shivering Nat was surprised at the way in which the Nez Perces ignored the yells and taunts from across the river. Their purpose, it seemed, had been accomplished when they saved the white men. Though they far outnumbered the Blackfeet and had fresh horses, they seemed indifferent to this chance to cross the river and score a victory on their ancient enemies.

Instead, they crowded around Captain Bonneville and his men with smiles and handshakes and earnest curiosity. They gave buffalo robes to the cold, wet men. The young brave who had ridden into the river to help Nat now gave Brent a hand to strip off the boy's soggy buckskins. He supplied his Hudson's Bay blanket, which had been on shore while he was in the water, with which to rub Nat dry. All the Nez Perces laughed at Nat's white skin. He was embarrassed to be, for the moment, without clothes. But he was not angry at the laughter, for he knew that was the Indian way of expressing interest or surprise. He wrung the water from his breeches and pulled them on but he slung the red blanket over his left shoulder as an Indian would.

The Nez Perces were not wearing their eagle-plume war bonnets. Their faces had only daubs and streaks of friendly red or yellow paint, not the harsh contrasts of black and white war paint. They wore loose buckskin shirts, belted at the waist. Many of these shirts had collars of rich brown otter fur, with the otter tail hanging in front. Shirts and leggins were heavily fringed.

Nat had noticed at once that these Indians wore their hair in two heavy braids, one on either side of their faces, much as did the Crows and Blackfeet. But unlike the men of those tribes, the Nez Perces did not part the hair on the front of their heads and draw it into the braids. It was cut off across their foreheads. With a few, it was drawn back in a pompadour.

Nat had expected another distinguishing—to him disfiguring—characteristic. He knew the meaning of *Nez Perce*, a French name, like so many other names of tribes and things and places in this country—Cheyenne, for instance, and Pen d'Oreille and Gros Ventre; parfleche, travois, butte, Teton, Lac Couer d'Alene. Nat studied the faces around him.

"I don't see any nose ornaments!" he whispered to Laramie.

"Nor me neither—never," answered the Canadian. "But de Sioux told de first traders these Injuns were *Tsupnit-pelun*—Pierced Nose, because long ago dey wore pieces of shell through nose. An' those traders, bein' French from New Orleans or Canayens from Quebec, turned de Sioux name into French, Nez Perce. These Injuns call demselves *Nu-mi-pu*—We People. But nobody else know it, or don't care."

It was a deep regret to Nat that he had lost in the river the rifle supplied him by Captain Bonneville. But his bow and quiver of arrows had come across safely, slung on his back. The Indians were examining these with approval. One of them drew the bow from its waterproof case of rattlesnake skin. When the Nez Perces saw that it was one of the fine horn bows made only by the bowyers of their own tribe they gabbled like geese. The one who was obviously their chief addressed Brent in the sign language.

"Well, I'll be hoss-kicked!" Brent ejaculated. "I knowed all the Injuns of the plains knew the hand talk but I didn't 'spose that any whose home is so far west o' the Rockies savvied it." He "threw the sign," as the Indians said it, that he understood.

Though Nat had not yet learned to "speak" much of the sign language he knew that it was far more than crude and improvised gestures. It consisted of over nine hundred symbols. It was easy to learn because the signs were descriptive, to a degree. But they were distinct and accurate. Indians whose homes were a thousand miles apart could talk to each other on sight as well as though they were from the same village—not just to tell their simplest needs but on any subject within the Indian range of thought. It was a means of communication between people of different languages more efficient than anything that white men, up to that time or since, have ever worked out.

"Where did your son get the Nez Perce bow?" Brent interpreted the question of the chief.

"From a Cutthroat who crept up to our camp to kill us in the night. The Cutthroat is dead," was the reply. Brent's hand drawn across his throat was the sign for Sioux. He did not consider it necessary to explain that Antoine Laronde, the traitorous deserter, was only half Sioux; or that he, Brent, had no son; that Nat was his friend only.

"Can the boy shoot with the bow of a warrior?" was the next question.

NEZ PERCE

"Ah, *mais oui!* But yes!" It was Laramie who here broke into—in fact, took over—the conversation. He rattled on in a mixture of French and Indian which the Nez Perces, judging by their grins and exclamations, understood. Laramie knew the hand talk, of course, but spoken words were quicker and more suited to his effusive temperament. When there was time to question him, Nat learned that Laramie, before he became a free trapper, had been a Hudson's Bay Company *engage*, that is, employee. This service had brought him from Canada down into the Kootenais and Spokane valleys, tributaries of the Columbia. That region was within the range of the far-traveling Nez Perces and he had learned to speak their language.

Laramie, with a self-satisfied grin, now repeated what he had said for the benefit of Captain Bonneville's party.

"I tell dem dat Big Medicine shoot wit' de horn bow as straight an' as strong—" he paused for emphasis, *"as any Injun!"*

"Haw-haw!" guffawed Tarno. But the captain and Brent exchanged looks of sober concern. Nat tried to protest. He knew the reckless conviction of Laramie's French-Canadian enthusiasm. The American mountain men exaggerated in pure fun. As: "Jim Bridger's been out here since Pike's Peak was just a hole in the ground." Or, "Yes sir, I found a peetrified forest with peetrified birds singin' peetrified songs in the stone trees!" But Laramie *believed* his exaggerations. He would be insulted by a suggestion that he take his statement back.

And, as Nat feared, there was an immediate challenge. The Nez Perces insisted that he show his skill. One of them dashed off on his horse to set up a target—his shield. The distance was about eighty steps.

Captain Bonneville tried to help Nat. He didn't want to see the boy humiliated—for Nat's sake or his own. To begin their relations with the Nez Perces by a boast that couldn't be made good would make the captain and all his band appear ridiculous. Dignity was of great importance in dealing with Indians. And at this moment the Blackfeet had left the captain with an unstable dignity—and nothing else.

"Tell the chief," he said to Laramie, "that the boy is tired from riding most of the night. That he is still cold from the river. Say that he will shoot some other time." Laramie put this into the soft-syllabled Indian tongue and translated the reply.

"Tu-eka-kas—dat's de chief's name—says young white warrior could shoot well enough right now, eef an enemy was shooting *at him*."

The captain tried to divert the Indians from their idea of a shooting match. "Ask Tu-eka-kas what he and his band are doing here, so far from their villages."

Laramie did not bother to put the question. "Dey goin' home from buffalo hunt. You know dis is de west line of buffalo country," he answered directly.

Still trying to get the Nez Perces to forget the notion of a shooting match, Captain Bonneville took off his hat. But the wonder of his bald head, that had so often proved fascinating to other Indians, failed to interrupt a lively discussion that had arisen over the horn bow. Tu-eka-kas finally announced the core of it, which Laramie interpreted.

NEZ PERCE

"De big man dey call He-me-ne Ilp-pilp—Red Wolf—he *made* Nat's bow. His mark is on it. Says it was stolen from him last summer at rendezvous. Says must be Nat stole it. Red Wolf goin' take it now."

Nat's face fell. Next to Pierre, who now was gone, the horn bow was the most valued thing he had ever possessed.

Captain Bonneville and Brent took the charge of theft as seriously, for a different reason. It was of supreme importance to have the best possible relations with these Indians, since the intended journey to the River of the West lay through the whole great width of the Nez Perce country. This accusation at the very outset of the trip was not just an ill omen. It was much worse.

"Among the Crows," Brent said, "stealin' is a joke, a skill to be proud of. Among the Blackfeet, it's limited to hosses—of their enemies. But with the Nez Perces, I've heard, it's one of the worst sins."

Laramie nodded emphatically.

"To give 'em the bow," Brent continued, "is easy. But it leaves 'em lookin' down their noses at us for cowards, or thieves—or both. How kin we prove to 'em that none of us stole the bow?"

It was the Nez Perces who supplied the answer.

"If the young white warrior can shoot with the horn bow as well as he has said," Laramie interpreted for Tu-eka-kas, "we will know he is honest. One who is honest could not have stolen the bow. Let him shoot now."

CHAPTER 5

Bowmen

Nat wanted to shout that he had not said he could shoot well with the bow; that *he* had not said anything at all! That it was Laramie who had let his admiration for Nat's ability—or his desire to brag—run away with him. Laramie had put him in this fix and Laramie should get him out of it!

But as Nat took the bow and arrows thrust into his hands, he realized that Laramie, even if he would, couldn't unsay what had been said—no more than anyone could undo the theft of the bow. Antoine Laronde, who had stolen it, was dead.

Neither could Nat remain angry very long at Laramie. Right now, the irrepressible Canadian was betting his Paloos horse against a clean-legged chestnut that the boy would win. To Nat, tense with the fact that the reputation for honesty of Captain Bonneville's party and the good will of the Nez Perces already was hanging on the outcome of this contest, adding a horse to the stakes gave him an uncontrollable impulse to laugh.

64

The sound of his own voice, laughing at Laramie's bet, shocked Nat. He knew that, except for the French Canadian's rifle, saddle and pouch of "possibles," which contained his fire flint, bullet-mold and pipe—things it would be *impossible* for a mountain man to do without— the splendid Paloos was all that Laramie had in the world. And it was easy for Nat to understand how the man cared for his horse. That realization drove it into him that there must be *some* foundation for what Laramie was risking. Laramie wasn't a dim-wit. It gave the boy his first hope that he could win—not the contest—but something more than ridicule; perhaps a measure of respect for his try.

Nat's laugh brought nods from a few of the Nez Perces. They thought it was a show of confidence—the thing the boy needed most. Their looks reminded him that, like an Indian, he must keep up a front.

He tried to set his face to hide all show of feeling. He fell to rubbing his bow as fast as he could. It had a backing of sinew. If any dampness had reached through its case while in the river, the heat produced by the friction of his palm would dry it. This was necessary if the bow were to have its greatest cast.

Seeing that there was no postponing this unequal contest, Brent and Captain Bonneville threw off their anxious looks.

"Don't worry, Nat. You're a better shot than you think," the captain said.

"But if they take my bow and Laramie's horse . . ." Nat stopped. He remembered that Captain Bonneville had just lost goods worth two thousand dollars—to the boy a fabulous sum—and fifteen horses!

65

"Nothing risked, nothing gained. Just you remember," the captain said hearteningly, "that the chap who does his level best—can't lose, no matter what score the other fellow makes. Breathe deeply. Take your time."

"Big Medicine, how about that new way of yours for drawin' the bow?" Brent asked. "Any advantage to you in that?" His low tone was earnest and for the first time it addressed Nat as though he were no longer a boy. Even more than the encouragement of Captain Bonneville, it steadied the thumping in Nat's chest.

"I *always* use that way now," Nat said. "For me, it's better than the Indian way—especially for a long shot."

"So I reckon! That last elk you killed at sixty paces. I pulled the arrow out by the head from the far side of him!"

The Nez Perces, after much talk among themselves, had chosen their marksman. It was not Red Wolf, though he had wanted to be the one to shoot. He was a powerful man, broad-chested and taller than any other in the band. Although Laramie's boast had been that Nat could shoot "straighter an' stronger than *any* Indian," a sense of fair play seemed evident in the Nez Perces—particularly in their chief.

"Tu-eka-kas says He-me-ne Ilp-pilp too strong to shoot against a boy," Laramie explained. "Big Medicine will shoot against Wookawkaw—Woodpecker." To Nat's surprise, this was the young brave who had ridden into the river to help him and Whitefoot reach shore.

In preparation to shoot, Wookawkaw pulled off his wet and clingy hunting shirt. This revealed a long cut across his left shoulder blade, from which blood had trickled to his waist. Nat remembered the wince that had crossed the Indian's face as he approached in the water and knew that this was the mark of a Blackfoot bullet. It had come within inches of taking the young fellow's life. But when Nat and Captain Bonneville showed concern over the injury, Wookawkaw laughed and strung his bow. A wound that did not cripple was to be ignored—at least, while a shooting match was on hand!

Tu-eka-kas explained, through Laramie, that Nat and Wookawkaw were each to have three trial shots to get the range of the target. Then five in the contest.

"Five is the Nez Perces' sacred number," the French Canadian added. "Not four, as wit' most Injuns. *Bonne chance!* Good luck!"

Studying the distant shield, which was the target, Nat wondered if the arrows would penetrate its heat-hardened parfleche deeply enough to stay where they struck. The very name *par fleche* meant "arrow warder," that is, shield. Because the Indian shields were made of rawhide, the mountain men had extended the meaning of parfleche to include rawhide in any way it might be used. On looking around him, Nat saw that the Nez Perce shields appeared to be lighter than those which he had seen the Crows make from the neck hide of a buffalo bull. They were elk skin, he guessed. One of these might make a target, though that meant it wasn't so much of a shield.

Anyway, the necessity was to *hit* it. It looked mighty small at eighty yards. Even so, Wookawkaw nicked it with one of his range-finding shots.

Woodpecker held his bow horizontally, drew it with a jerk and released instantly. That was the customary way among Indians, who hunted mainly on horseback. Watching closely, Nat saw that the Nez Perce used the "draw" or hold upon the arrow and bowstring that was also used by the Crows.

Nat did not know it, but *all* North American Indians pinched their arrows between thumb and first finger as they drew a bow. Since only a man with a viselike grip in his hand can draw a powerful bow by this method, the Indians of some tribes put knobs on the notch end of their arrows to give a better hold. Most of the buffalo hunting tribes devised a way of strengthening the "pinch" draw by bending their fingers until they brought the tips of either the first and second or the second and third to pull also upon the bowstring. This had been taught Nat by Far Eagle.

It was a cramped position of the hand and had seemed awkward to the white boy from his first lesson. He was of a methodical nature and "snap" shooting did not come naturally to him. Brent had thoroughly trained him to take deliberate aim in shooting with a rifle. But even the cedar bows the Crow boys used were too strong for Nat to draw, by their method, and hold for an aim.

He'd done the best he could, which wasn't very well, until he came into possession of the Nez Perce horn bow that had been found in the dead hand of Antoine Laronde. This bow had been too strong for the boy to shoot at all, using the Indian draw.

However, Nat had no centuries-old traditions, as the Indians had, to hold him to their method. He had experimented until he worked out a way by which he *could* draw the horn bow the full length of an arrow; a draw of his own.

It was *his* draw, so far as Nat was concerned, and he would probably never know otherwise. But it was the draw that had been used by European archers since the beginning of history—and by people as remotely scattered over the earth as the Eskimos of the Arctic and the Igorrotes of the Philippines.

Instead of holding his arrow between thumb and forefinger, Nat folded his thumb into his palm and did not use it at all. He held his arrow between his first two fingers and drew the bow with three fingers pulling directly on the string. The fingers were straight, except for their tips. They did not, as in the Indian draw, lose part of their strength by being curved and more of it by a needless pinch upon the arrow. Nat had practiced his method until he could hold even this powerful horn-and-sinew bow, drawn, for a quick aim.

He made his range-finding shots.

The vertical position of Nat's bow was not unusual and brought no comment. But the keen-eyed Nez Perces saw the hold of Nat's fingers on the bowstring from his first trial shot. He heard their whispers of surprise that there *was* a draw different from their own. How surprised they would have been could they have known that all the bowmen of Asia, from the hordes of Genghis Khan and the Turks who whipped the Crusaders, to archers of China and Japan—have drawn the bowstring with their *thumb!* But then the Indians would have been surprised, probably no more and no less, to know that a continent of Asia existed, although their remote ancestors crossed Bering Strait from there.

Keen as their interest in the contest was, the Nez Perces were a courteous audience. They made no distracting comments. Wookawkaw shot first. The flight of his arrows arched high, but all five were hits. They stuck in the shield.

Nat's eyes remained on the target but he heard an approving release of breath from the watching Indians. "Beat that!" he could sense them thinking. He stepped into the tracks in which Wookawkaw had stood to shoot.

The chill of the river had not entirely left Nat. There was the chill of tension as well. He tried to use the advice Captain Bonneville had just given him, to breathe deeply and think of nothing but to do his best.

But thoughts raced through his head like a herd of horses. The thought of how much depended on his placing of these five arrows. The wish that Far Eagle were here to shoot for him. Far Eagle! Last night he'd been glad that Far Eagle was *not* with him, in the danger of the chase. Now he wished with all his might that he *were* here—in the safety of this band of Nez Perces, instead of being alone in Blackfoot country.

Nat's thoughts swirled on. Since he must go through with this contest, it would be much easier for him if he believed, like an Indian, that he had a totem—a personal "medicine"—to help him.

Medicine? Why, Brent in fun and Laramie in earnest, called him Big Medicine. Supposing there *was* something in the idea, what would be his totem? What in all nature did he care for most? Horses, of course. A horse like Pierre, who by his sense and agility had saved him from the charge of a wounded buffalo. A horse like Kiowa, double-loaded but running away from the Blackfeet. Even one like White-foot—not so much horse and worn to strings—but still doing the best he could.

The best he could. There it was again! Nat's thoughts had run without a bridle all the way 'round his horizon and were back at the start. His best was all he *could* do. But he'd make sure to do *that*.

He had selected his five straightest and most evenly matched arrows. They were Crow war arrows he had picked up on the battlefield in the Tetons. He fitted one to his bowstring and at the same time filled his lungs. He raised his bow and, as he brought it downward, he put all the toughened muscles of his fingers, arms, shoulders and back into his draw upon the sinew string, until he anchored his folded thumb against his jaw—held rocklike for a brief but unhurried aim. Released. Not with a flip, but with a straightening of his finger tips as steady as a rifle marksman's squeeze of his trigger.

"*Zing!*" sang the bowstring, joyfully.

The arrow sped, more flatly than those shot by Woo-kawkaw. It struck the shield. The "Ah!" of surprise that broke from the throng of Indians and the tingle of satisfaction that went through Nat upset him just enough to make his next arrow scuff the ground at the target's edge. He steeled himself again. His remaining three arrows hit.

Laramie and most of the Nez Perces threw themselves

on their horses and scurried to the target in a clatter of
hoofs and swirl of dust. But Tu-eka-kas walked the distance
deliberately beside Captain Bonneville. Brent and Nat and
the older Indians followed. Thronged around the target
but careful not to touch the arrows with which it bristled,
the hundred or more Indians seemed to be all talking at
once.

"*Sacré!*" cried Laramie above the racket. He grabbed
Nat's arm. "You miss heem once but you hit heem twice
mos' near de center! An' all your arrows cut clean t'rough
de parfleche. Wookawkaw's arrows jus' stick good into it."

Nat knew that much of the credit for the greater pen-
etration of his arrows was due to some Crow arrow maker
for the patient art he had put into his slender, sharp flint
points. Now that he was close to the arrows of Woodpecker, he could see that they were hunting arrows. They
had heavy shafts to balance their heads, which were wide,
for greater shock on antlered elk and ponderous buffalo.

The reason for the Nez Perces' noise was the question of
who had won.

Had a bull's-eye and concentric rings with set scoring
values been previously drawn on the shield, it could now
be determined accurately whether Nat's four hits totaled a
higher score than the five hits of Wookawkaw—provided
the Indians were that mathematical. But as it was, even
though Tu-eka-kas did much measuring with a twig, he
finally spread his hands palm up to indicate a balance. He
spoke judiciously.

"De chief say," interpreted Laramie, "dat it was also
claimed de young white warrior shoot *strongly*. He says

Big Medicine and Wookawkaw will each shoot one more arrow. Shoot almos' straight up, when he give de word. De one whose arrow falls *last*—dat feller wins."

Nat and Wookawkwa stood a few feet apart, facing away from the crowd, for the falling arrows must not endanger anyone. Now there would be no question of aim—only strength—of the bowmen and of their bows. And in bows Nat was sure he had an advantage. The greater weight of Woodpecker's hunting arrows was not *all* of the reason for the higher arc of their flight to the shield. Part of the reason why Nat's had gone more swiftly and flatly was because the bow in his hands, made by the muscular Red Wolf, was a stronger bow. If Nat, now, could just use it to its full advantage . . .

And the difference in weight of arrows was also in Nat's favor. In a "flight" or distance shot like this, his lighter arrow was an advantage so great he was surprised that none of the Indians had protested it.

He reminded himself how much he needed that help. Didn't Wookawkaw have an advantage of five years or more in age and thirty pounds in weight? Tu-eka-kas wasn't blind, nor foolish. Perhaps the Nez Perce chief liked him because he, Nat, had done better than anyone expected. So, if the chief chose this way of giving him the decision—wasn't it all right? "Shut up," Nat told his conscience. "Shoot!"

And then he stepped over to Wookawkaw. He held out one of his light Crow war arrows.

Laramie's face went blank. Some of the Indians grew owl-eyed in surprise. Nat heard Tarno growl in disgust.

73

But Wookawkaw's ready grin spread to his ears. He took the arrow. He ran his tongue along its shaft, then drew the moistened shaft across the daub of red paint on his cheek, thus marking his arrow with a red smear. A lift that was unexpected went through Nat. This was a *contest* again!

The pair fitted their arrows and raised their bows toward the belly of a white cloud that drifted across the blue above them.

"Shoot!" said Tu-eka-kas.

Both of them drew their bows to the length of their arms or the limit of their strength. The bowstrings sang together. The arrows flew.

There was a breathless time that stretched unbelievably. *Thunk!*

"One-two-three-four-five—" counted Nat.

Thunk!

A Nez Perce runner pulled from the sod the arrow that had struck last. He raced with it to the chief. While everyone stared, Tu-eka-kas held it above his head. It was the one *without* the red paint.

Then Captain Bonneville and Tu-eka-kas were shaking Nat's hand. Brent was gripping his shoulder. Laramie was thumping the breath out of him and talking in French, English, Nez Perce, Ojibway and maybe Blackfoot and Cree. But still it stayed in Nat's mind that the sky beyond that white cloud toward which he had sent his arrow was the *bluest* sky he had ever seen!

Hungry Trail

In the valley beyond the ridge where the shooting match had taken place were at least two hundred more of the Nez Perces' horses, under the care of guards. Scouts along this ridge had seen the approach, beyond the river, of Captain Bonneville's desperate party and the pursuing Blackfeet.

About half of this horse herd was extra mounts to be ridden on the trail so that the strength of the fastest horses could be saved for running buffalo. But the rest of them carried packs, proving that the buffalo hunt of the Nez Perces had been successful. The packs, Nat soon learned, were composed mainly of hides—fine skins of cows and young bulls. Robes were more valued by these Indians than leather for tepee covers, so they purposely held their annual hunts late in the fall, when the buffalo were well furred.

The Nez Perces were packing less buffalo meat than Nat expected. The trail was far too long, Laramie explained, to carry meat still fresh to their homes, even in cool weather. Besides, this country of the upper Snake River was claimed either by the Blackfeet or the Shoshonies, so the hunt was too dangerous for the Nez Perces to bring their women with them to dry the meat.

"Which don't mean dey let it go to waste," said Laramie. "Dey take plenty of time wit' hunt, choose an' kill only de best buffalo, dry some of de meat for trip home, eat de rest."

Nat had seen Indians—and mountain men, too—eat buffalo roasts in unbelievable quantities. After riding all day, he could do well at it himself.

Captain Bonneville now found an opportunity to dress the wound on the shoulder of Wookawkaw. He then smoked with Tu-eka-kas and told the chief of the trade goods he had cached before he started into the Blackfoot country. He explained that the cache was two days' travel upriver. If the Nez Perces would wait here, the captain promised to return soon with presents and with goods to trade for horses. He wished also to travel with them toward the River of the West.

But Tu-eka-kas said that it was too dangerous for his people to wait. The Blackfeet would be almost certain to attempt night raids on their horse herd. Or they might gather an overpowering war party. Now that the chief was convinced that the captain and his men spoke with straight tongues and did not steal, he would gladly let them have fast horses which they could pay for when they returned from the cache. The small band of white men could travel with more secrecy and speed than his large company of

Indians and their many horses. Surely they could overtake the hunting party farther down Snake River.

"Anyway," he concluded, speaking through Laramie, "The Chief-who-has-been-scalped and his son, Strongbow, will be welcome at the Nez Perce villages."

Again it was not explained that Nat was not Captain Bonneville's son, either. But the boy knew it didn't matter, for Indians often used the terms father, son or brother to mean any relative or close friend. And he was acquiring, he thought, as many names as a typical Indian. "Talks-with-horses, Big Medicine, Strongbow!" He recited them to himself, not a little pleased.

Laramie insisted on giving to Nat the chestnut horse he had won by his bet on the boy's shooting. Nat, through Tu-eka-kas, tried to give it to Red Wolf, to replace his loss of the bow. But the chief and the bowyer both refused the offer.

"Strongbow did not steal it; he must not pay for it. When another great ram of the *he-yets*—the bighorns—is killed, He-me-ne Ilp-pilp will make another bow."

Nat's bay, Whitefoot, was turned loose with the extra horses of the Indians. When the captain and his men had smoked with the chief and headmen of the Nez Perces long enough to meet the requirements of Indian courtesy, their new horses were caught for them and they rode eastward. The Indians filed away to the west. Toward evening of the next day, the captain and his party reached the first of his caches.

"Cache," Nat knew, came from the French *cacher*, to conceal. But when used here in the mountains, it might mean to hide oneself, to hide things of value, or the place in which the valuables are hidden. A cache in the Indian country had to be made with great care. First a well-drained spot of ground had to be selected, so furs or cloth stored there would not mildew from dampness. It must have a good cover of sod. From an area two feet across, the sod was cut in large pieces and saved. Then a hole six to ten feet deep was dug, growing greater in width as it went down. All the dirt removed from the hole was carried on a hide or blanket and thrown in some nearby stream, where the current would wash it away. Unless the pit was dug in firm clay, it was cribbed with poles to prevent a cave-in. In any case, it was lined with hides or dry grass.

When the goods had been stored to within two feet of the surface, a cover of poles was laid on the cribbing or on stout shoring so that even a horse might walk over it. Stones were packed over the wooden cover to prevent coyotes from digging in. A layer of grass was spread on the stones and finally the sod was replaced. The original appearance of the spot was restored with such care that the owner of the cache might even need to record notes and measurements of its location to find it himself when he returned, weeks or months later.

Since the leader of any large trapping or trading party could not trust all of his followers completely, the job of making caches put much effort on the few in whom that leader placed confidence. Brent, Tarno, Laramie and Nat had done all the work of making Captain Bonneville's two caches, for the captain had taken the added precaution of not putting "all his powder on one pack horse," as Brent expressed it. They now found that this had paid off. One cache had been found and robbed. This was a hard loss which seemed all the more severe, coming as it did on the very heels of the losses in goods and horses to the Blackfeet. But it was not such a disaster as would have been the case if all that the captain possessed had been in the one pit.

"*Au Diable!*" stormed Laramie. "An' I brush all de grass on dis knoll wit' pine bough to straighten it from our trampling! Somebody mak' strong medicine an' talk to hawk dat watch us from de sky. Dat's how he find cache!"

"Medicine yore hind leg!" said Tarno. "That Crow kid was in our party when we made the caches. He wa'n't supposed to leave camp but he prob'ly spied. Then he told the place of the cache to his *tilicums*—relatives—that night the Crows hit at us. The young 'un was gone for hours, remember? You kain't tell when this happened, 'cept that it was before the rain four-five days ago."

The slur against Far Eagle made Nat's blood run hot but there was no use storming at the hard-shelled Tarno. The thieves had been bold enough to ignore covering their trail but the rain Tarno referred to had so nearly obliterated it for them that even Brent and Laramie gave up trying to follow it.

Captain Bonneville took everything from his undiscovered cache. The quantity of goods put heavy loads on their five extra horses but the captain would not now risk leaving part of it.

At a spot some ten miles farther upriver where he had agreed to meet the fifty men who made up his several trapping bands, the captain left a message. It was carved on a slab of aspen and it informed the "partisan" or lieutenant in command—a man named Fenton—that the captain was starting at once for Oregon. It told him to hold the men in a winter camp in whatever part of this region would provide the best pasture for their horses and sufficient buffalo for their own food supply. The captain would, the message said, join them here before they dispersed into the mountains for the spring beaver hunt.

Placing the message in the fork of a conspicuous tree, Captain Bonneville and his companions turned their horses down-river. Westward, at last! was the meaning of Nat's long breath. The only cloud in his sky was that Far Eagle and Pierre were not with him.

Nat's new chestnut was a handsome horse, hardy and quick. Though not as easy-riding as Pierre, he gave signs of being as fast a buffalo horse as he was claimed to be. But he was a typical Indian horse, which meant that he was accustomed to being mounted from the off side, instead of the near, and used to being guided by a horsehair cord looped around his jaw. With a bridle, he was hard-mouthed and he tossed his head and champed his jaw endlessly at the bit. Indians prized their horses for their appearance and speed. They might spend hours decorating them with paint and feathers and weeks of patient effort in training them in usefulness. But, as a rule, Indian horsemen were liberal with the lash, did not talk to their horses or pet or reward them, and so did not develop any affection in the horse for his master.

This chestnut had a particularly independent nature.

Besides being unresponsive to Nat, he was indifferent to Kiowa and Laramie's Paloos and showed but little interest in the other Nez Perce horses. Generally, he grazed on the edge of the herd and never whinnied for the others if they went over a ridge or if he were ridden off on a scouting duty. "Call him Kosooyeen," said Laramie, "Dat's Nez Perce name. Means 'Going Alone.' And," he added significantly, "picket him stoutly at night."

Always conscious of the nearness of the Blackfeet from whom they had so narrowly escaped, Captain Bonneville and his party maintained their usual caution. They traveled at the limit of the strength of their loaded horses, yet they did not overtake the Nez Perces. Two days' journey westward from the place where they had left Tu-eka-kas and his men they saw, in the sky ahead of them, buzzards circling.

Ordinarily, the sight was not unusual. Buzzards were always over the ground where a successful buffalo hunt had been staged. But now the party was west of the range of the buffalo. Nat had an ominous feeling as they followed the Indian trail into a broad canyon.

There they came upon grim evidence of an ambush and battle.

A number of dead horses explained the buzzards. Broken arrows and lances, and Blackfoot as well as Nez Perce shields were scattered over the floor of the canyon. But any warriors killed on either side had been carried away by their comrades for proper burial. Captain Bonneville and Brent studied the battlefield gravely.

"It may have been a sharp loss to our friends," concluded

81

Brent, "but it wa'n't a knockout. Their trail is still that of so many hosses you kain't tell if forty or so were taken from them."

"Me, I bet you they don't get licked," said Laramie. "Nez Perces don't begin many fights but dey fight like *hohots*—their name for grizzly bear—w'en somebody start a fight wit' dem!"

The truth of this might have been a lesson re-learned by the Blackfeet, for there was no sign that they followed the Nez Perces. But the Indians from the west had, from here on, traveled in "long camps." That is, in long stages between camps. Captain Bonneville's party tried to do the same, but with no extra horses upon which to change loads, they could not keep up with—let alone overtake—the hurrying Nez Perces.

Unlike the Indians, who were homeward bound from the buffalo country, the captain's party had no supply of dried meat or other provisions. The long hours they spent on the trail in these shortened days of early winter left little time for hunting. Worse, there wasn't much to hunt.

The country through which they passed was growing constantly more arid and rocky. It was volcanic in origin. Lava flats were cut by innumerable ravines. The only large game that existed here was a few antelope, but it was seldom that anyone in the party could get near enough to one for a shot. Southbound geese passed over them in tantalizing numbers. They shot one occasionally on the river and secured it at the cost of a cold wetting. But one of these when divided, made small servings for five persons whose normally large appetites were increased by semi-starvation.

The river was full of fish—dead fish, for the salmon that each summer ascend the Snake River, and all northern streams flowing into the Pacific, die after spawning. Brent killed a bear by the river. The joy which the whole party felt over this apparent stroke of luck was short-lived, because the bear, for a long time, had been living on the dead fish. Only by smoking and roasting its flesh until the meat was charred could any of them but Tarno choke a little of it down.

"Meat's meat," said Tarno, a common expression of the mountain men, referring to the unusual and unsavory things they were sometimes compelled to eat to keep alive.

The nights were freezing now and the winds across these rough plains cut like a knife. Gray skies and frequent snow squalls were anything but cheerful. The wild geese were gone.

Grass had for a long time been scarce, and even willows for browse. It hurt Nat more than his own hunger to see their horses grow ribby and rough haired. Their hoofs had worn short on the stones. Several of the animals limped. There was no buffalo hide to lace over the horses' feet, as Nat had seen the Crow Indians do when traveling in rocky regions.

The westerly course of the Snake had turned and it was a surprise to Captain Bonneville that for many days they had been moving northward. As the weather grew colder, the snow squalls no longer melted. One storm covered the ground to the depth of a foot. The Indian trail they followed could no longer be readily seen. They had no fear of getting lost. They told themselves there was always the river. But as higher and higher hills crowded the Snake and more and longer detours around canyons became necessary, it would have helped greatly if the Indian trail had still been plain before them. Blundering out a route for themselves was costly of time and strength—their own and the rapidly failing stamina of their horses.

"Those lyin' Napercys promised to wait fer us," growled Tarno. "But ye kain't never depend on a Injun."

"They did *not* promise to wait!" Captain Bonneville corrected him. His tone was sharp. It was natural that the tempers of all of them had grown thin. "Their chief said we could probably overtake them. But the attack of the Blackfeet gave them good reason to speed up. When they entered these barren hills, it became impossible for them to wait because there is so little forage here for their many horses."

"It's *their* hosses that cleaned out the little feed there was—so that *ours* are starvin'," Tarno grumbled, resentful still.

The little party struggled on, stopping at any place where they found sere bunch grass sticking up through the snow or a stunted cottonwood, or a patch of willows whose twigs had not already been bitten off to coarse stubs of indigestible wood. They would fell the tree so that their horses could bite the bark from its smaller limbs. For themselves, the men were immensely thankful for a sage hen or a rabbit. In dividing these, Brent tried to favor Nat but the boy protested and even flatly refused portions which he knew were Brent's own share.

Three days after the snowstorm, they reached a place where the hills that had been crowding the river suddenly grew to mountains that forced the stream into a wild gorge. Captain Bonneville spent much of his diminished strength in climbing to a high shoulder of the nearest mountain. But he brought back to camp the news that he could see nothing ahead of them but a jumble of peaks.

They knew that, in the deep dusk of the previous evening, they had passed a campsite of the Nez Perces. An open flat by the river had suggested that this might be a place where the Indians had stopped, and Brent's exploring feet had turned up freshly charred stick-ends from under the snow. So the captain's party had groped on down-river in the darkness, to find for their horses forage that had escaped the hungry Indian herd. Therefore the trail must still be near!

But this morning neither Brent nor Laramie could find any sign of it—no faint depression in the snow over a path scuffed in the gravel by many hoofs, no cropped willows or cut cottonwood.

"We'll have to make our own way," concluded Captain Bonneville, staring again at the forbidding mountains. "And the outlook isn't promising. We must again cache most of this stuff we're packing. And kill a horse for food."

Nothing Nat could think of seemed worse.

To spend the time and strength necessary to dig the usual pit for a cache here where the ground was mostly rock, was out of the question, especially when there was

85

such need to hurry on before starvation overcame them. So the men separated to search the nearby gulches for a cave or at least an overhanging rock that would protect the goods from the weather. To hide the things did not matter so much now. As Laramie explained, the few Indians who came through this region were mostly Nez Perces and they would not molest a cache.

Nat herded the horses. Their search for browse was poorly rewarded . . . a wisp of frosted grass here, the twigs of a scrubby willow there, or a bite of bitter sage. Since he could go no farther down the river, he drove the horses slowly back in the direction from which they had come. He speculated miserably on which horse would be killed. The one most lame, he thought, and under these grim circumstances least valuable for riding, which, thank goodness, wasn't Kiowa. But it *was* Kosooyeen, his aloof chestnut. Going Alone had split his near front hoof badly. Just when Nat, after weeks of patient effort, was beginning to make friends with him!

It came to the boy's mind that he might drive Kosooyeen away from the other horses and let it appear that he had strayed during the night. Perhaps no one would remember having seen the chestnut this morning. But Nat knew that mountain men were sharply observant and had good memories. And it would be almost as hard for him to see any other horse killed in Kosooyeen's place.

Dreading this, he drove the horses farther than he realized in their search for the scanty browse. He wished they were on the other side of the river. Over there, he could see a grove of cottonwoods whose bark would make

86

a good fill for the horses' empty bellies. He was brought up in surprise by his arrival back at the Indian campsite which they had passed at the edge of dark the night before.

Nat pictured the open flat, not more than three nights ago, gleaming with campfires and populous with friendly Indians whom they were so eager to overtake. But that only deepened its loneliness now. A little snow was falling, silently. The broad river, still unfrozen, was black from reflecting the dull sky and by contrast to its white shores. It flowed swiftly in an eerie stillness, intent on its own purpose and indifferent to the troubles of Nat.

More startling to him than a shot, there came from the other shore a human voice in a long call.

He stared through the thin veil of falling snow and saw a man on the gravel bar across from him. The man waved and called again. Nat answered, eagerness giving his voice a sandy feel in his throat. The man pushed into the water what Nat thought was a log lying on the gravel bar. It was a dugout canoe. He caught up a paddle and began stroking vigorously. By heading well into the current, he came almost directly across. He landed where Nat waited for him.

"Strongbow!" he cried, and leaped ashore.

Only one person Nat knew could grin so broadly. It was Wookawkaw—Woodpecker—against whom he had shot with his horn bow.

Nat had learned from Laramie perhaps a hundred words of Nez Perce, while from Brent a little more of the sign language, the "hand talk." So he was able to understand that Wookawkaw had waited here to act as guide to Captain

Bonneville and his party, because at this point they must cross Snake River. The villages of the Nez Perces were in the pleasant valleys of the Imnaha and Wallowa rivers, beyond the forbidding mountains that flanked the Snake on the west side. But the first of those villages was only "four sleeps" away!

"So that's what became of your trail!" exclaimed Nat. He looked at the black river and shivered, especially as he remembered the canyon less than two miles downstream. Then he eyed the hollowed and pointed log doubtfully. But he was too glad to see Wookawkaw to begin worrying. The craft must be one that the Indians kept at this place to aid them in their occasional crossings. Only the horses of Nat and his companions would have to swim, and this time they would be unburdened and on lead ropes behind the canoe.

His next thought was that it was no longer necessary to cache the trade goods. They could be ferried, too.

"I must find the captain!" Nat cried. He leaped on Kiowa, strongest of the horses and, leaving the others under the eye of Wookawkaw, rode back to their own camp and out into the hills. By whistling and calling he soon found the four men. He told them the good news.

Once again Laramie praised the strength and sureness of Nat's "medicine."

"But I didn't *do* anything!" Nat protested. "I just followed the horses. When we got back to that flat, Woodpecker saw us." But to Laramie this only proved his point —that Nat's medicine guided them to good fortune.

Wookawkaw soon explained, through Laramie, that he

88

had waited for them on the other side of the river because over there was the grove of cottonwood trees. They understood well enough the importance of firewood, shelter— and bark for his horses. He had four with him, in case they were needed. The captain's one gesture toward his ribby and limping herd was a reply that stronger horses were needed very much.

Then the Indian's face expressed great mortification. "I tell you *three times*," he said, "that I watched close for you and I did not see you pass!" Laramie explained that to say a thing three times was a Nez Perce guarantee of truth, like "cross my heart." The first or the second time, one of the tribe might make a statement jokingly or give an evasive answer. But it was a sin as black as stealing to make any misrepresentation more than twice. Wookawkaw's grin broke wide as ever when he learned that, contrary to custom, Captain Bonneville's party had traveled some distance in the dark the evening before, so missing them wasn't negligence on his part!

He was asked the outcome of the battle with the Blackfeet. Again his moonface clouded, this time with genuine grief. The Nez Perces had repulsed their attackers with, he said, "great losses." But he showed no elation over it. Three of their own best warriors had been killed. Seven, including Chief Tu-eka-kas, were wounded. It was not in fear, he said several times, that the Nez Perces had traveled so fast since the battle. It was because their wounded were more likely to recover at their homes with the aid of their *te-wats*—their medicine men. Or, should they die, that they might be buried in the land they loved, the Wallowa Valley.

The name, Laramie explained, meant "Winding Waters."

The ferrying began. Nat and Brent crouched in the canoe, each holding the lead-rope of his horse. Nat's dealings with big rivers had all been of the wrong sort to develop a love of them. There was the time he had been kicked off the river steamer, *Indian Belle*, into the muddy Missouri and was pulled from the swirling water by a boat hook. That was his introduction to Captain Bonneville, who had fished him out. Again, the raft on which they were ferrying wagons had gone to pieces and spilled him, the loaded wagon *and* the captain into the rain-swollen Kaw. He had seen horses and wagons stuck in the quicksands of the Platte. And swimming the Snake River, a month ago, with the exhausted and frightened Whitefoot was not a memory to inspire confidence. Still, he could remember that each time he in some way got out!

Right now it was alarming—and yet faintly comforting —to look at Brent. Nat's most admired mountain man wasn't enjoying this either. By his puckered look, Brent would rather have chanced the river on Kiowa, gaunt as he was, than in this tricky log canoe.

But Laramie picked up the extra paddle as gladly as though it returned him to his boyhood, which, in memory, it undoubtedly did. Even so, once they were out in deep, swift water, Nat felt the greatest admiration for Wookawkaw for his skill in steering the long, loaded craft and the zest of his fight with the current. The white boy

remembered that, when he was among the Crows, he had
heard them speak of certain Indians living a long ways to
the west as the *Apupé*. In Absaroka that meant "to paddle." Far Eagle had since then told him it was the tribe
the white men called Nez Perce that the Crows called
Apupé. Now Nat saw why.

It hurt Nat that the bony horses had to endure the gripping cold of the water. But they made it to the farther
shore. There he and Brent vigorously rubbed the animals,
and did the same for each succeeding pair that scrambled
up the river bank. Laramie and Wookawkaw made four
more trips to get all the horses and goods across.

Then what a meal they had of the dried buffalo meat
Wookawkaw supplied!

CHAPTER 7

Medicine Man

Even with Wookawkaw to show the way, Nat and his companions soon found that crossing these mountains was to be a bitter test. The trail was steep. As they climbed, it became more deeply blocked by snow. Men and horses had been strengthened by recent food but it takes time to recover from semi-starvation. It was now that they learned how weak they really were.

The packs that the horses carried had been lightened by distributing part of the load to the extra horses of Wookawkaw. To save their saddle horses, the men walked much of the way. They took turns breaking trail. They stopped often. Their progress was slow and grim.

The work of climbing was not all that sapped them. Often the footing under the snow was only sloping rock on which the horses slipped and fell. Repeatedly, they had to be helped to their feet. The higher they climbed, the more often the trail skirted yawning gulches and canyons. Nat had crossed such places in the Tetons—and still shuddered when he thought of them. But that was in summer, when there was no snow to obscure the footing. To him, the test of nerve was more wearing now than the test of strength.

Greater still, to a person as sensitive as Nat, was the pain of seeing their horses strain and pant and stumble; of watching shrunken muscles quiver and matted hair that was wet with sweat, freeze in the winter wind. There was timber up here to shelter the camps they made but most of it was fir or spruce. Its twigs and needles were too resinous and bitter for horses to eat. The beasts kept alive on the twigs of a few willows and on the bark of aspens which the men cut for them each camping time.

Wookawkaw's supply of dried meat soon vanished down the throats of six persons made wolfish by toil and cold. Deer lived in these mountains but the snow had driven most of them to the lower valleys. By watchfulness and luck, Brent sighted a small buck across a canyon. By patient stalking and expert shooting, he killed it and by breath-robbing work, he brought the dressed carcass across the gash of the valley and up to camp. Again they feasted, thankfully, though snowflakes flitted through the firelight and the wind soughed in the firs above them and rumbled in the gulches below.

For four days they plowed and plodded, up and up and up. When they went downhill for a short spell, it was resentfully, knowing they were losing elevation they must regain at even greater cost. One horse died of exhaustion. One fell a thousand feet into a canyon from which it was impossible to recover even the packs. The men had frosted fingers, toes and faces. They spent themselves until they were almost insensible, then slept like logs in their buffalo robes until they were routed out by the cold to replenish the fire and be ready, at daylight, to stumble on.

But at last they found they were going steadily downhill. Now the snow was growing less deep. The air became much warmer as they advanced. Then they were out of the snow entirely. There were dry ferns and leaves for the horses to eat . . . and then small meadows of rank grass. The west side of the mountains was much warmer than the east side. A chuckling stream of water beside them grew rapidly to a small river.

"Imnaha," said Wookawkaw. "*Taats!*" (Good.)

An Indian wearing fringed, beaded and clay-whitened buckskin and riding a black and white horse of splendid build and spirit met the gaunt and ragged party. He exchanged a few words with Wookawkaw, wheeled his horse and galloped away. An hour later he reappeared and ceremoniously handed Captain Bonneville a horn of gunpowder. This, Laramie explained, was an official token of welcome from the chief of a village they were nearing. It was to make sure they could return the salute of firearms from the village, in case their own ammunition was low.

Captain Bonneville called a halt beside the stream and the white men shaved and washed their faces and combed their neglected hair. Pride of great obstacles overcome raised their sagging shoulders. They had crossed the Snake River Mountains in winter! Food and rest were near! The captain opened his packs and gave to each of his men a bright-colored shirt, so that the band might make a better appearance at the village.

Nat called the captain's attention to Wookawkaw, who was eyeing this distribution of finery from a distance. For an Indian, Woodpecker had always had a rather shabby look. Nat had learned to disregard it because of the fellow's unfailing good nature. How he had withstood the cold of the high mountains in his greasy buckskin and tattered blanket had been a mystery to the white men—except for the fact that during the month previous he had been better fed than they.

"He's a Injun," they said. "He's tough." And if he looked like a redskin ragamuffin, they decided it was because he didn't care.

But now there was a wistfulness on Wookawkaw's round face that made him calf-eyed.

"I've planned to reward him," Captain Bonneville said, "for his big help to us. But I thought I should make my presents to the village chief first. However, that look is irresistible."

So he gave Wookawkaw a scarlet shirt, a dark blue blanket, a hatchet to thrust in his belt and a pair of silver discs to wear on the braids of his hair.

Woodpecker lost not a breath in adjusting to this elegance. He took a good look at himself in a quiet place in the stream and his moonface became a rising sun. He strutted and clucked like a sage cock in springtime. Then he leaped on his horse and tried to make the tired animal do a pirouette. It couldn't, but Wookawkaw rode out ahead of the band.

The travelers passed around a grove of trees and saw the welcoming committee, consisting of all the men of the village, riding out to meet them. All were in ceremonial dress, even eagle-plume headdress. On their many-colored horses, they repeated the swift and intricate drill with which they and their comrades had made themselves known the time Nat first saw the Nez Perce hunting party. There was much banging of fusees, aimed skywards. It was not for the noise alone that they did this. An *empty* gun was the symbol of a peaceful purpose. The captain and his men replied with several volleys.

The picturesque cavalry halted. The village chief and a few headmen rode forward to meet Captain Bonneville. Wookawkaw, caught off base in the lead position, sidled around this group of important persons to mix with friends of his in the rear rank. It was days before Nat saw him again.

The chief was a man with streaks of white in his hair. He had not been with the buffalo hunters. He introduced himself as Hin-mot Toot-si-kon, or Speaking Thunder. After much handshaking, a custom learned from traders, he designated those of his followers whom he considered of sufficient importance to accompany the guests to the council lodge. Others he appointed to unpack and unsaddle the visitors' horses, guard them while they grazed and be responsible for the safety of the visitors' goods.

Nat's eyes were wide and the first thing to strike his attention was that most of the Nez Perce lodges, instead of being cone-shaped like those of Plains Indians, were oblong in ground plan and many times as large. Some were more than a hundred feet long. Two ridge-beams upheld them and the long, narrow space between these beams was left open to admit light and allow the escape of smoke—not the smoke of one fire, as in a tepee, but of ten or a dozen fires in a row—one for each two families that occupied the communal dwelling. There was but one door on each side of the house. The lodges were not covered with skins but with mats woven of tules and tied in place shingle-fashion. There were a few conical lodges but they seemed to be for councils or for the entertainment of guests.

When all were seated in the order of their importance, tobacco and red willow bark were cut on a birch board and mixed, and a long-stemmed pipe was filled and lit. Smoke was offered to the Earth-mother and the Sun-father and then the pipe was passed around the circle of men in the direction in which the sun appears to move around the earth. When a proper silence had passed, to make sure that no one spoke without first considering his words, Speaking Thunder asked about the captain's journey from the buffalo country.

Captain Bonneville answered in some detail, mentioning the goods he had brought as presents and to trade for furs. He told again of his intention to follow the River of the West to the big trading fort of the "King George men." He acknowledged his indebtedness to the Nez Perces for protecting him and his men from the Blackfeet and thanked them for detailing Wookawkaw to guide the party through the mountains. He expressed sorrow for the warriors killed by the Blackfeet and asked about the wounded ones.

He was told that one had died . . . that Tu-eka-kas was still very sick . . . that the rest had recovered.

The home of Tu-eka-kas, the captain was informed, was

in the Wallowa Valley, one day's journey from the Imnaha. But the chief had been too exhausted by the trip over the mountains to go farther than this village. His squaw, his son and the *te-wats* or medicine man from his own village had come here to care for him. The *te-wats* name was Tip-yah-lah-nah—Strong Eagle. No eagle's eyes, it seemed to Nat, could be more stern than his were, under their thick brows.

Captain Bonneville explained that he was something of a medicine man himself. This was readily credited because word of his treatment of the slight wound of Wookawkaw had preceded him. He asked to be taken to the wounded chief, suggesting that Strong Eagle accompany him. He was rather surprised at the *te-wats'* agreement. The captain declined to eat first. He got his kit of surgical instruments—his medicine bundle to the Indians—and took Nat with him, as usual, as his orderly. Laramie, of course, came as interpreter.

Tu-eka-kas was in one of the conical lodges apart from the rest and they walked to it rapidly. The sun had gone behind the next range of mountains westward. The chill that had immediately come in the still air held the tangy smoke from the lodges in a blue veil near the ground. Axes could be heard, and voices, but they did not seem to disturb the peaceful stillness. What Nat noticed most distinctly was the near and far tinkle of horse bells.

He knew that Crows and Blackfeet used bells for parades and ceremonies only, never for the mere convenience of making it easier to find their horses. Bells would be just as helpful to an enemy. But Plains Indians seldom knew

98

such an unguarded evening as this, with no threat of war.

The wounded chief lay on a bed of buffalo robes, spread on a mat of tules. His features were so gaunt Nat would not have recognized him. His squaw, a handsome woman whose heavy braids of hair reached below her waist, and his son, a sharp-eyed boy of ten or eleven, watched the entrance of the white medicine man anxiously.

The wound was in the chief's chest, on the right side, just below the collarbone. It was that of a bullet. There was no opening in his back. The wound had not closed.

Captain Bonneville's brow knitted gravely.

" 'A little knowledge is a dangerous thing,' " he quoted, half to himself, half to Nat and Laramie. "I've plunged right over my depth and placed us all in a predicament. If I do nothing, I'm a no-good medicine man. And with that bullet in him, the chief is pretty sure to die. I don't know why he *didn't* die, coming over those mountains! But if I try to remove the bullet and *then* the chief dies, I may be blamed for his death—with who knows what consequences to all of us."

He continued pondering his decision in silence. Nat saw the sunken black eyes of Tu-eka-kas fixed on the captain calmly, even confidently. The captain saw them, too—and he opened his kit. He took out a slender forceps. This fascinated Strong Eagle by its shiny appearance.

The captain had Laramie explain to the *te-wats* how he hoped to remove the bullet. The medicine man agreed that it would be a good thing to get the bullet out. But it would be very difficult, he said, for the bullet *could not* be an ordinary one of lead. He, Tip-yah-lah-nah, had given

Tu-eka-kas a charm which, combined with the power of the chief's *wyakin* or protecting spirit, made it impossible for bullets or arrows to pierce his body. Everyone knew this was so. Tu-eka-kas had been through many previous battles without harm. Therefore this must be a medicine bullet of horn or bone which the shiny fingers could not catch.

He consented, though, for the white *te-wats* to try. He even agreed to help. Nat wondered how.

Captain Bonneville asked for a pitchwood torch, to better light the lodge, and for hot water with which to wash his instruments, his hands and the area around the wound. The wife of Tu-eka-kas, whose name Nat learned later was Yi-yik-Wa-sum-wah—Swans-lighting-on-the-water—brought these silently. There was great appeal in her large, dark eyes.

Laramie was told to place himself ready to hold the chief's arms and prevent him writhing in the pain that was sure to wrack his body. Nat was given the torch to hold. The captain stripped off his shirt and scorched it over the torch to have something ready to absorb blood and to bandage the wound. With a thin metal probe, he located the bullet.

But the forceps had to be spread to grip the bullet, which was of at least .50 caliber. They slipped off again and again. The disturbed wound bled. Nat found he was holding his breath until it broke from him in near-gasps. He saw perspiration shining on Captain Bonneville's bald head and even on the brow of the usually careless Laramie.

But Tu-eka-kas never moved, nor opened his pressed lips. There had been times—too many times—when Nez

100

Perce warriors had been cut slowly to pieces by outnumbering Blackfeet. Not one was known to have disgraced his tribe by making a sound other than a defiant war cry. Their chief could do as well, now.

His burning eyes were fixed on something behind the captain. Nat, glancing up, saw that it was a grotesque medicine doll in the hand of Strong Eagle. The other hand of the *te-wats* shook a weirdly carved rattle, while from his throat came a guttural, unvarying sound. Loud as it was, Nat had been too tense to know when it began. It seemed to go on endlessly, without a break for breath. Strong Eagle was making medicine to fight the evil in the bullet. Nat guessed that if the chief believed this strongly enough, perhaps it *did* help Captain Bonneville—at least by helping the chief to hold still.

The forceps was drawn out at last and between its points was a battered bullet. Unquestionably it was lead. But Strong Eagle did not blink or show a flicker of surprise when the captain dropped its solid half-ounce into the *te-wats'* hand. The captain covered the wound.

The next day, with Tu-eka-kas still alive and even improved a little, Strong Eagle was showing through the village a bullet he said he and the white *te-wats* had taken from the chief's chest. It was one carved from buffalo horn.

Captain Bonneville said nothing to the contrary. Nor did he ask Tip-yah-lah-nah three times if what he said were true.

"Perhaps his story is best," the captain remarked to Nat and Laramie. "Before Strong Eagle or anyone else destroys the Indians' faith in charms and *wyakins*, he should have something to put in the place of it. He is generously saying that *I* make strong medicine, instead of telling what he knows of how scared I was while I was tugging on that bullet—or mentioning the fact that any man who could go through what Tu-eka-kas did last night without a move or a murmur—that man is just too tough to die."

CHAPTER 8

Horn Bow

Food and rest, for themselves and their horses, were the first needs of Captain Bonneville and his party. The horses were turned loose in the wide, fertile valley. Though they shared it with hundreds of Indian horses, the autumn rains had sprouted new grass and there was enough for all. Nat asked at once about Whitefoot. He was told that the little bay had stood the long trail and scant feed as well as any of the Indian horses. Before turning Kosooy-een loose, Nat secured from the Indians a small piece of buffalo hide which he soaked in water and, with Brent's help, laced in a tight boot over the split hoof of the chestnut. A steel shoe was what was needed—had been needed for a month on the hoofs of all the horses. But the nearest steel shoes were at Fort Osage on the Missouri, 2,000 miles away.

The captain and his crew were quartered in one of the conical lodges. Feasts were given in their honor every night. These, with the smoking and talking that followed, lasted half the night. The captain presented gifts. He had much to ask; about his route to the River of the West, about the Nez Perces and their customs. Also about their neighbors, the Cayuses, Yakimas and Umatillas. Would these Indians trade with him if he returned and set up a trading fort in this region?

This brought an uncertain answer. Even the Nez Perces, friendly as they were to the captain and pleased with his presents, felt a certain loyalty to the Hudson's Bay Company. This great British company, by treaty between the United States and Great Britain, enjoyed equal trading rights with Americans in the vast and indefinite region called Oregon until the ownership and boundaries of the territory should be agreed upon. But the Hudson's Bay, already more than one hundred sixty years old, was here first and had treated the Indians with a patriarchal fairness for many years.

The Nez Perces had even more to ask about the Americans. What were their numbers, their customs, their religion? Were they all brave? Were they all as generous as the Chief-who-has-been-scalped? Why, after these twenty-five years, had not Lewis and Clark, whom they loved, returned to visit them?

But even with feasts, the white men were hungry, for a large portion of the Nez Perces' diet at this time of year consisted of the dried roots of the kouse plant and the bulbs of the camas lily. The latter grew so abundantly in these valleys in summer that the prairie was blue with its blooms. The Indians had dried salmon but were sparing of it, for their supply was small. The salmon run of the previous

104

summer had been light. The muscular bodies of the Nez Perces proved that their food was wholesome. But the diet of the mountain men—when they'd had a diet lately—had been entirely of meat. Camas, whether as soup or as meal cakes, was, to them, "not tough enough under the belt."

When Captain Bonneville tried tactfully to suggest to their hosts that his men would like something else to eat the Indians assured him by example and by words that camas was *"Taats,"* good. To show dissatisfaction by trying to buy meat might give offense. To go out to hunt for themselves was of little use, for game had become very scarce in this region where so many Indians lived and hunted during the greater part of each year.

A solution to the food problem came through the captain's quickly acquired reputation as a medicine man. When he was offered payment for his services by the many Indians who came to him with ailments of various sorts, he always asked a fee in dried salmon. This met the approval of all but Tarno.

"Fish don't shine with me more'n onct or twict a week," he grumbled still. "Prime cow buff'lo, now—or even poor bull—this man kin eat an' *like* ev'ry day the sun comes up."

The captain's "medical practice" brought problems, too.

"I really want to help these people," he said to Nat and Brent. "But my few drugs are simple and my experience is limited to watching army surgeons and helping them in emergencies. I can set a broken bone and sometimes extract a bullet, but for many ailments the *te-wats'* treatment may be better than mine. He knows useful herbs and the value of Indian sweat baths and certainly he knows the ways of the Indian mind. I don't want to arouse his jealousy by taking his patients away from him. He's been their doctor, sorcerer and adviser and could turn their belief in his supernatural powers into serious trouble for us."

The captain took Strong Eagle with him whenever he called on Tu-eka-kas.

The chief was improving slowly. To supervise the care of him was one of Captain Bonneville's reasons for remaining at Speaking Thunder's village. Another reason was for trade. But the principal one was in order that his men, he and his horses might regain strength.

Nat, with the natural comeback of youth, was ready for action the first of anyone in the party. Curiosity took him all around the village. His reputation had run ahead of him and, wherever he went, he was greeted as Strongbow —and made welcome.

This gave his lively eyes a chance to compare the customs and skills of the Nez Perces with what he had learned of the Blackfeet and Crows. He saw quickly that these Indians possessed many similarities to the Indians of the Plains, and at the same time striking differences. They were ardent horsemen—but they were also fishermen and canoemen. They liked meat, but an important part of their diet was roots. The Crows ate roots—if they could get them—*only* when there was nothing else.

Nez Perce men made war bonnets of eagle-plumes, shields of parfleche, ornamental breastplates of bird-bone beads; all in the manner of the Plains Indians. But no coupsticks bearing scalps were hung before their lodges. They preferred peace to war.

Plains Indian women went bareheaded, or pulled a robe or blanket over their heads in cold weather. The Nez Perce women wore attractive little hats, without a brim, that were woven of grass. The women of this tribe, Nat noticed, did not cut their hair across their foreheads, as the men did.

Nez Perce skill in weaving was notably different from the ability of the Crows and Blackfeet who, so far as Nat had seen, made only a few rough baskets of willow twigs. These Nez Perce women wove the tule mats that covered and floored the lodges. They made baskets of all sizes and sorts. Into their hats and the choicest baskets they wove decorative patterns of grasses that had been dyed.

In all their clothing, these Indians showed a desire for decoration equal to that of the Indians of the Plains. The dresses of the women were made of two excellently tanned deerskins, sewn together over the shoulders and down the sides. They were always fringed and often embroidered in many-colored floral designs. For this, dyed porcupine quills were used to some extent, but more often glass beads. The moccasins worn by both sexes were richly beaded as were the cuffs and side-flaps of the men's leggins. Saddle skirts were beaded, too.

Such extensive use of beads Nat had not seen before. That, Laramie explained, was because the Nez Perces did most of their trading at posts of the Hudson's Bay Company, which brought its supplies from Europe, where these small beads were made. The American Fur Company and

Rocky Mountain Company bought their goods in the United States and had not yet included beads, other than large ones of the necklace type, in their stock in trade. So, of the Plains Indians, only the Blackfeet, who usually fought the Americans and did their trading in Canada, had embroidery beads in any quantity.

Laramie did not have the inclination to be Nat's guide for more than one turn around the village. Whether the white boy needed a guide or not, another was at hand. It was the intent-eyed son of Tu-eka-kas. He followed Nat like his shadow.

Probably he had heard enough about Strongbow to win his admiration. Certainly he had seen Nat act as assistant to the white medicine man who had saved his father's life. Nat borrowed Brent's rifle for long enough to offer the boy a chance to shoot at a stick thrown in the river. The youngster came nearer to it than Nat expected. From there on they were friends.

The boy's name was Wa-chum-yus. By a swing of his arm to indicate an arc across the sky and by pointing to one after another of the colors on his beaded shirt he made Nat understand its meaning—Rainbow. He took over where Laramie and Wookawkaw had left off in teaching Nat to speak Nez Perce. The quickness with which Nat had learned the Crow language from Far Eagle made him all the more adept at gaining a working vocabulary in this soft-spoken tongue.

Rainbow, though himself only a visitor in this village, led Nat freely in and out of every lodge. Every lodge but one. He took Nat to where the men were raising tall posts to support the ridge poles of a new lodge. He explained that Wayakat—Going Across—who was one of the warriors wounded in the battle with the Blackfeet, was with them no longer. The lodge in which he had died must be torn down. That was the one not entered by the boys.

The widow of Wayakat and two other women whose husbands had been killed in the battle were pointed out to Nat. They had cut their long hair at the neckline. They would not, Rainbow explained, be allowed to marry again until their hair grew below their shoulderblades. The tails of Wayakat's horses had been docked and they would not be ridden until two snows—winters—had passed; that is, all of his horses but the five best. Those had been killed on his grave so their spirits might go with his, because, for a Nez Perce, it would be a disaster to be on foot, even in *Ah-kun-ken-e-koo*—the Land Above.

Next the two friends visited the place by the river where the women were beginning the long task of dressing the buffalo skins brought by the hunting party that had recently returned. Since it had been Nat's duty to help the squaws tan hides for tepee covers when he was a prisoner of the Crows, he was particularly interested in Nez Perce tanning. He found their method to be much the same, except that these women were making robes, instead of leather.

The dried skins had been soaked in the river just long enough to soften the hides but not to loosen the hair from them. Spread over logs, they were scraped with an elk rib into which a toothed strip of hoop-iron had been set. Scrapers of stone or beveled leg bones had been used be-

109

fore the traders brought hoop-iron in their ships that came to the Columbia River's mouth.

When every bit of flesh, fat and tissue had been removed from the skin, it was rubbed with a mixture of grease, the brains of an elk or deer, the inner bark of some tree—and usually some secret substance which the tanner's *wyakin* told her to use. As the skin dried, it was kept soft by stretching, twisting and rubbing. This, as Nat well remembered, was just plain hard work. Making robes, he could see, was even more difficult than making leather, for the hair added to the weight and bulk of the skin. But how soft and warm the finished robes were!

Rainbow, who had been fidgeting while Nat watched and asked questions, now led the way to his rabbit snares and the deadfalls he had set for mink and otter along the river. The trapping ground allotted him by the other boys was not the best and fur was scarce, anyway, near the camp. Today he had no catch. But two of his deadfalls had been sprung and the bait stolen. Rainbow pointed to broad, long-clawed tracks.

"*Carcajou!*" Nat exclaimed, for the French-Canadian name of this trap-robber was more common than the English. "You'll sharpen your wits, Wachumyus, to catch him!" he prophesied, recalling the many stories he had heard the mountain men tell of the devilish cunning of the wolverine.

"We call him Skunk-Bear," Rainbow explained. "He will eat anything, like a skunk. He has a smell something like a skunk and looks a little like one. But he is large as a

110

cub bear and strong as a half-grown bear and more brave than an old bear, or panther or wolf."

Patiently Rainbow reset his deadfalls, using the one rabbit his snares had yielded for bait.

They were led farther down the river by a growing sound of rushing water until they reached a place where the Imnaha tumbled and foamed between huge rocks. Platforms of poles had been built above the stream. Rainbow went out on one of them quickly and confidently, followed gingerly by Nat. Because of the noise of the water, Rainbow used signs to say that in summer, when the salmon run was on, the men of the village fished here.

Even as they stood there, the younger boy pointed quickly to a slim shadow in the white water below a rock. Nat glimpsed it. Then it was gone. Rainbow's black eyes glistened and he led Nat ashore. From a roofed cache he took two long-handled dipnets. Their hoops were made of willow, their meshes of corded cedar bark. Words tumbled from Rainbow faster than Nat could interpret but he got their drift.

The run of steelhead was on!

Steelhead, which are trout that go out to sea, came mostly in winter—never in such numbers as salmon. Some of them grew longer than a man's arm. This was earlier than the run was expected. Rainbow and Nat, new to this village and almost strangers to this river, were first to discover that the fish had come.

They took stations on the platforms. Still as stones, they watched the white water. An hour passed. Nat's expectation was slackening. He began to think they had imagined the shadow in the water. His eyes shifted to Rainbow. As suddenly as a steel trap, the Indian boy dipped. Lifted. His net writhed and gleamed at the surface of the water. It took all of his strength on the long handle to bring to the platform the big trout.

They waited again for a long time. The sunlight became slanting. Nat's spurred interest was not lagging but his power of attention was wearing thin. A fish jumped to an amazing height above the frothing water, snapping him back to the alert. He saw two beneath him in quick succession; dipped for each, but missed. Rainbow caught a small one. Nat dipped the full length of his handle at just the hint of a shadow below his rock and felt the thrilling jerks of a great struggling. At the surface, the weight of the fish bent the net handle alarmingly. Nat had his catch halfway up to his platform when the net, untested since the previous summer, broke. The white river gulped the trout and the pole and empty hoop swung high in Nat's disappointed hands.

Rainbow was as certain as Nat, while they carried their two fish home, that his friend's steelhead that got away was the biggest one that ever swam up the Imnaha.

The early steelhead run was big news in camp. Nat and Rainbow were at the rapids at daylight the next morning but every fishing station was occupied by men of the village. The boys watched while a few fish were landed, then took the heads of the two caught by Rainbow the evening before and re-baited and reset the deadfalls. In one was the body of a mink, its skin slashed past any use by the wanton claws of the wolverine.

The tracks of the marauder showed more plainly in the soft earth this time. The Indian boy pointed to one of them significantly. Looking more closely, Nat saw that the track was that of the right forefoot and that from it the inside toe was missing.

"Been in a steeltrap!" Nat exclaimed. "That means he's come a long ways—from where white men are trapping. It means, too, that you'll be old before you catch him!"

"All skunk-bear wander," said Rainbow, "like spirits of dead warriors who are never buried. And all are *te-wats*. But soon I shall have a *wyakin*. It will tell me," he finished with patient confidence, "how to catch this skunk-bear."

Back in the village, Rainbow scraped the fish he had caught the day before with what Nat thought was an unusual thoroughness. The boy explained that he was gathering a substance from which glue was made. It was obtained only from the skin of steelheads. And only one glue was stronger. That was made by boiling the blood of a sturgeon. Sturgeon were huge fish, sometimes weighing nearly as much as a horse. The Nez Perce caught them only in the Kah-mu-e-nem—the Snake River—and rarely at that. So steelhead glue was even used sometimes in making the horn bows.

"*How* are the horns made?" Nat asked. Ever since he had owned one he had put that question to anyone he even guessed might know. No one had been able to tell him, other than that it was from the great curling horns of the mountain rams, called *ahsatah* by the Crows, *he-yets* by the Nez Perces.

Rainbow's reply was simply, "I show you." He caught a pair of Indian horses which they saddled and rode to the village of Circling Swan, three hours' journey away.

"He-me-ne Ilp-pilp live here," Rainbow said. "He kill big *he-yets* two suns ago."

They found Red Wolf, the bowyer, in a sunny spot between tall pines. He greeted Nat with the usual exclamation, "Strongbow!" And a quick smile which removed the white boy's anxiety that Red Wolf might resent the loss of the fine bow which Nat possessed. But the tall Indian tapped approvingly the bow now slung on Nat's back, with its panther skin quiver of arrows.

Before them lay the head of the great ram. Nat caught his breath at the magnificence of the specimen. The immense, curled horns made it as impressive to him as the shaggy, bearded head of a bull buffalo. And of course it was far more rare and a hundred times harder to secure. With a thong of buckskin, he and Rainbow measured one horn, around the ouside of its spiral from its base to its tip. Then they held the length of the thong at Nat's shoulder. It nearly touched the ground.

"All of four feet!" exclaimed Nat—though that meant nothing to the two Indians.

Red Wolf pointed out that the horns were not split from fighting nor their points broken off in indication of great age.

"Make good, lively bow," he said.

With an obsidian knife and wedges and mallet of oak, Red Wolf began cutting and splitting a wide strip from the outside of the curve of one horn. It must continue for the horn's entire length. Patience and the greatest care were required to keep the strip from breaking, scaling, running narrow or being weakened in any way. Much of the time the rough edge of the stone knife was used as a saw.

"I'll come back next summer to see you finish it," Nat said.

But he came back every day, except once, when he had a turn on one of the fishing platforms. He found that Red Wolf made remarkable progress, considering the tools with which he worked.

When the strip of horn was cut out and roughly dressed to an even width, it still retained its spiral curl. A trough had been hollowed from a short log. Red Wolf filled this a third full of water and built a fire in which he heated many stones. With sticks for tongs, Nat and Rainbow helped him pick up the stones and drop them into the water. A cloud of steam rose. The strip of horn was hung in the stream, and then the trough was covered with a blanket.

The horn bowstave was stretched, testingly . . . steamed further by the addition of more hot rocks to the water in the trough . . . stretched again. Finally it was lashed, inch by inch, to a straight stave of oak.

During the days when the horn was drying, Red Wolf showed the boys how he made arrows. Shafts of green serviceberry bushes were heated, straightened and set in a frame, to hold them until dry and hard. They were smoothed with a rasp of tufa, a soft, volcanic stone. Arrowheads were worked from obsidian by a patient flaking off of the glasslike stone under pressure of a spike of deer horn. One end of the arrow shaft was split. The head was then inserted in the cleft and bound there with sinew, which was then coated with glue. The other end was knotched and three vanes of split feathers were glued to the shaft, to hold the arrow steady in flight. Each warrior who bought these arrows would paint his own identifying marks upon the shafts.

The horn bowstave, now dry, was removed from the oak straightener. It was worked down to an even thickness and a gradual taper toward each end. The tools used were stone scrapers and rasps. Again and again, the bow was strung and tested during the process. What had been the inside of the horn was now the outside or back of the bow, which added to its spring. To make this spring even greater, long, flat sinews, which had been taken from the backs of buffalo or elk and dried, were now glued, layer after layer, to the back of the bow. For this, Red Wolf had a little block of the dried sturgeon's-blood glue, which, when moistened with saliva, was ready for use. The sinew backing was built up to a thickness as great as that of the horn and a cover of rattlesnake skin was glued on this, to keep moisture from softening its strength.

The horn or belly side of the bow was now polished with ashes, then with oil and the palm of Red Wolf's hand. He performed ceremonies over the bow which he did not explain to Nat but which the boy knew were believed to give it a charmed accuracy, at least in Red Wolf's hands. His mark—the same strange little curlicue that was on the bow Nat carried, was cut into it. Then the new bow was tasseled with black-tipped white weasel tails, taken from Red Wolf's medicine bundle—and was ready for use!

116

Of course, they set up a target; one made of many layers of tightly woven tule mats. Nat found the new bow stronger than his own. Even with his three-finger draw it was quite beyond his strength to draw it until the bowstring reached his jaw. Red Wolf experimented with Nat's draw, clucking to himself over its novelty. He admitted its strength. But like Far Eagle and all other Indians who had seen it, the method seemed too different from the one they had used since boyhood and which their fathers, no telling how many generations back, had been taught was the *right* way to draw a bow. He could hit nothing by Nat's method and laughed and gave it up. Nat, too, had to admit a difficulty with his draw, in that it made his fingers sore after a few shots.

Those few shots proved again to the crowd of Indians that had gathered that Nat was remarkably accurate and strong for a boy not fully grown. But the sureness and swiftness of the arrows shot in turn by Red Wolf made Nat more than ever glad that it had *not* been against the powerful bowyer he had contested, that day by the upper Snake River. Nat silently renewed his gratefulness to Tu-eka-kas for giving him a sporting chance and appointing Wookaw-kaw as his opponent. Woodpecker, he now knew, was just a better-than-average shot—not as good as Far Eagle. He would like to see Far Eagle shoot against Red Wolf. He would like to *see Far Eagle* . . . anytime, anywhere, anyhow!

With an effort, Nat recalled his thoughts from the buffalo-hide tepees huddled in a snowy grove of leafless cottonwoods along Tongue River, or some other frozen

117

stream back in the country of the Absaroka—the Crows—the country which Far Eagle was so certain was "in just the right place." And where Far Eagle now was—Nat hoped. He brought his mind again to this lazy afternoon by the sunny Imnaha. But he followed the Crow custom and gave the arrows he had used in this contest to Red Wolf, who had beaten him.

The Nez Perce bowmaker took Nat's Crow arrows with deep chuckles of pleasure. Who could appreciate better than he—master craftsman—the nicety of their balance and their artfully made points of red flint, contrasting with his arrow-heads of black obsidian. In parting, he gave Nat the stone knife with which he had so laboriously cut the ram's horn.

He promptly took up a point of deer horn and began to flake out another knife, to cut the other horn of the great ram to make another bow!

Nat and Rainbow mounted their horses and rode back to Speaking Thunder's camp. Nat knew that this was the last time, for he had heard Captain Bonneville say they would start soon for the Wallowa. He realized that he had witnessed what few if any white men had seen, the making from start to finish of a Nez Perce horn bow. And since guns, with the one advantage of a little greater range, were taking the place of bows so fast among the Indians, the boy had an unhappy thought that what he had seen was something few men, red or white, would see again.

As he rode, Nat still carried his own bow in his hands. He was trying to estimate how much more he valued it, now that he knew the amount of Red Wolf's effort, skill and patience that had gone into it. Suppose he added also the months it had taken to find a bighorn ram with horns large enough to make a bow like his. And the days or weeks of stalking and waiting among the cliffs and snow-fields to get the wary old flock-leader within bow range— the skill to hit him mortally; the strength and nerve to pack him down glaciers and not go headlong, along preci-pices and across slopes of loose rock!

Nat concluded that, even though he did not have a *wyakin* or medicine that he could call on, he had a great deal of Red Wolf at his command, whenever he fitted an arrow to his horn bow.

119

CHAPTER 9

Wolverine

It was decided that Tu-eka-kas could now be moved to his home in the Wallowa, the Valley of Winding Waters. Although the chief declared he was able to ride his horse, Captain Bonneville had a travois made for him. A long pole was tied on each side of a horse, with the ends resting on the ground. Behind the horse, spreaders were lashed across the poles and a robe was stretched over this frame. On this the chief might lie in fair comfort.

Strong Eagle, who had assisted in these preparations, now took up his medicine bundle and mounted his coal-black horse. The horse which drew the travois was led by Swans-lighting-on-the-water. As befitted the chief's wife, she was riding a horse which Nat admired as much as the Indians did. It was a black-and-white, as evenly marked as Brent's pinto was in white and red. Little bells tinkled on the beaded skirts of the saddle which, like all the saddles of the Nez Perce women, had a high pommel and cantle of elk antler.

The Indians had rounded up the horses of Captain Bonneville and his men. All the animals had regained strength and spirit remarkably. Kosooyeen, Nat's chestnut, had nearly recovered from his lameness, but the boy saddled Whitefoot. The other horses had all been packed. Everyone was eager to be on the westward trail again.

But Speaking Thunder now spoke at length. His deeds as a warrior in times past and his love of the white men were reviewed. Over and over he mentioned the honor they had just received by a visit from the Chief-who-has-been-scalped. The horses pawed and the men fidgeted. At last the chief finished by saying that he was now too old for the long trail to the buffalo country, with its wars and hardships. And, since Captain Bonneville's horse was entirely unworthy of him, he, Speaking Thunder, would give the great Chief-who-has-been-scalped his own best war horse.

The horse was led forward. It was truly a good one; pure white, the color most preferred by Indians because it could be painted to suit any occasion.

Captain Bonneville, pleased but a little puzzled, told the chief, as briefly as ceremony would permit, how honored he was by the gift. While he shifted his saddle to the white horse, Nat heard him whisper to Brent, "Is this pure generosity? Or does he want to cut in on the attention we've been paying to Tu-eka-kas, his neighbor chief?"

"Better take it as a Injun gift," Brent advised him.

The captain, at the beginning of his visit, had made presents to all the men of importance in the village. But he now gave Speaking Thunder a rifle. Here, so far from where it was made, it was worth two of even the best of horses. But that fact did not prevent the old chief from quickly drawing forward a very wrinkled and sad-faced squaw.

"My wife loves the white horse," Speaking Thunder said. "When he is gone, she will not be able to hold up her head."

Captain Bonneville opened one of his packs and found a gift of a pair of large red ear-bobs. The old woman put them on at once. Half her wrinkles vanished and she was able not only to hold up her head but to cock it with a ridiculous pertness.

The captain had his hand on the mane of his new horse and his foot in the stirrup when the chief pushed forward an Indian who wore the longest face Nat had ever seen on a Nez Perce.

"My son has cared for the white horse since he was foaled," said Speaking Thunder. "He has trained him and loves him more than a brother." Wearily Captain Bonneville returned to his pack and found a hatchet and a knife to soothe the son's torn heartstrings. Again he tried to get his party under way.

"I tell you three times that I shall always keep this gun," said Speaking Thunder, with the rifle held above his head. "By it I will remember the great and generous Chief-who-has-been-scalped. But with some powder and lead and percussion caps—since this is not a flintlock—I could also kill deer with it, which would be an advantage. . . ."

The captain did not go to his packs this time but quickly gave the chief the powder horn and bullet pouch he was

122

wearing. He swung to his saddle and spurred the white horse beyond the range of Speaking Thunder's speaking. But he was laughing when Nat overtook him.

"Hin-mot Hih-hih—White Thunder," he said, naming the horse, for the Captain had also been learning Nez Perce. "I, too, will keep *you* near me as the gift of the most dignified beggar I ever knew, a delightfully human old *bag of wind!*"

They traveled steadily across prairie and through woodland. By a pass through a narrow but rugged range of mountains they reached the Wallowa at the end of the day. Here were wider prairies and they were dotted with horses, the wealth of the Nez Perces. Timber, black with shadows, followed the streams. A few lakes blazed golden under the sunset.

The undemonstrative Brent surprised Nat by an exclamation. "What a long, rich furrow a man could plow here! An' wouldn't this hoss like to turn it!" The meaning of this grew as it penetrated Nat.

The boy had already half-forgotten that, before the death of Brent's wife Sarah, his friend had been a thorough, if restless, farmer. Their cabin had been the only civilized home worthy of the name that Nat had ever known. And yet, so fast had this far western country and Indian life changed the boy, that a furrow seemed the *last* thing he wanted to see here. To him, it would be the most deadly threat to the valley's present peace and beauty, so he could hardly believe it was Brent, his ideal of the foot-loose, adventurous mountain man, who was talking of furrows

. . . dreaming of fields whose fences shut a man on one place!

If it was peace Brent sought, Nat could in part agree with him. But the peace the boy wanted was best expressed by smoke that drifted from lodge tops and from campfires that didn't need to be hidden. Brent, Nat suddenly knew, was picturing smoke that curled from solid chimneys and hung in a pall over cleared woodland.

Nat could find no reply. But he was still brooding over this sudden difference in values between himself and his oldest friend when they were welcomed to the village of Tu-eka-kas. Below the lodges, stars were reflected in the chilly waters of the Wallowa.

The white men would spend a few days in trading. Rainbow, fully at home here, was Nat's guide and companion, with even greater self-assurance than before. He lost no time in taking over his line of deadfalls from Es-pow-yes, his older cousin.

Es-pow-yes meant Light-on-the-mountain. The Indian boy had been through the vigil in which he received his man's name and learned his *wyakin*. It was clear to Nat that this experience took place at an earlier age among the Nez Perces than among the Plains tribes. There it had more to do with proving a candidate's fitness for the war trail. Sometimes, as in the Sun Dance of the Blackfeet, it involved tests of enduring pain that would give a man scars to be proud of for the rest of life. Far Eagle was older than Nat and he had only passed his test and obtained his man's name and his totem during the previous summer. But here Rainbow, who was not more than eleven, was eagerly awaiting the event. It would be whenever his father and Strong Eagle said the time was right. Among the Nez Perces, many girls took the vigil also. Es-pow-yes told Nat a good deal about it, but all details he must keep secret.

He then showed Nat and Rainbow his three captive eagles. He fed them rabbits and kept them tethered with thongs of parfleche that was too hard for even their strong, hooked beaks to cut. Two of them he had captured before they were fully grown and had carried them down from their nest in the top of the tallest pine on the nearby mountains.

But the other had the proud white head of an eagle that for years had been lord of the sky. Es-pow-yes had caught him by hiding, day after day, in a covered pit, with a captive fawn tied within arm's length. At last the eagle had dropped like a thunderbolt out of the sky and seized the fawn. Instantly the boy had gripped the legs of the eagle. In some way he had withstood the blows of the bird's powerful wings and had thrown a piece of buckskin over its head. But his arms still showed the scars of its beak and talons.

All of the eagles had been plucked once of their largest feathers. By a tribal rule, when their feathers had grown out again, Es-pow-yes might pluck the birds a second time, but take only a few feathers. Then the eagles must be released.

The boy could have traded the plumes he now owned for many valuable things, but he was saving them for the day when he would make a headdress to wear in the dances and parades of his tribe. By the charms worked into it, this

125

was expected to protect him should he ever need to fight the Shoshonies or the Blackfeet.

Nat asked Rainbow if he, too, would soon begin to catch eagles.

"Yes, if my *wyakin* tells me. But I would rather become known to my people for some other thing." The boy paused as though wondering whether he would be understood, then said earnestly, "When I look at the eye of an eagle who is tied to the ground, something makes me feel that *I* am tied in a cave. The eagle cannot forget that he was made to ride the wind, just as I could never forget that I was made to ride a horse in the sun."

Nat asked for Woodpecker, since this was his village. Light-on-the-mountain smiled and shook his head. "Wookawkaw not here," he said when Nat pressed him. "He is never long in one place." Nat guessed there was some reason why he did not want to say more, so asked no further questions.

On the second day that Nat and Rainbow ran the deadfalls, there were four sets sprung and torn to pieces, but nothing had been caught. As at the sets on the Imnaha, there were wolverine tracks. Rainbow pointed to one—and Nat stared. There was no mark of an inside toe.

"Skunk-Bear followed us," Rainbow said. "It is like I told you; he is a bad, lost spirit." This time the boy did not reset the deadfalls. He only put up the baits, to keep the wolverine around.

The next day Rainbow did not come to Nat's lodge and when the latter went in search of him, the boy's mother explained that today Wa-chum-yus was to seek his *wyakin*.

Nat saw the chief's son being led by Strong Eagle to the bath hut for purification. This, he knew, would consist not only of a steambath produced by pouring water over heated stones but of a ritual by the *te-wats*. It was useless to inquire about this. Later in the day, he saw Rainbow, with one blanket but no food, weapon or fire flint, go alone toward the wooded mountains.

Nat had been alone in the hills and knew how big and empty they could be—even though he had enjoyed the company of his horse, Pierre, which had made a great difference! All the rest of that day he thought about Rainbow, trudging through the still woods, climbing to some designated place. Perhaps it would be above a cliff, perhaps in some grim canyon. When he reached it, he would begin his prayers to Hun-ye-wat, the Great Spirit, to send him the spirit with the qualities he most desired. He would dance the dances his father and Strong Eagle had taught him; would dance until he dropped!

The spirit that came to him and instructed him in his sleep would be his *wyakin*, his totem. If he obeyed it, it would guide and protect him throughout his life.

The spirit of *Hohots*, the grizzly, was that of strength and courage in war, *At-e-mis*, the spirit deer, could give him swiftness. *He-me-ne*, the wolf, was the great hunter; *Itsi-yiyi*, the coyote, was the clever one. *Hin-mot*, thunder, was the mightiest and most mysterious power in the world.

From something in his dream or some circumstance of his vigil he would choose his name. That would be his real name, though he might be known by many others for his deeds later on. And if no dream came? Then he must

127

continue, perhaps for a week. Or perhaps the vigil must be repeated at a later time.

The second day of Rainbow's absence, Nat borrowed four beaver traps from Captain Bonneville, who took them from his stock of trade goods. Following Laramie's instructions, Nat rubbed them with grease and smoked them above a fire to destroy the man scent on them. He smoked a pair of mittens, too, and put them on before he touched the traps. He waded down along the edge of the river, leaving no scent as he approached the location of each of Rainbow's deadfalls.

It took all Nat's weight on the double springs of the traps to set them. He placed them carefully, secured their chains and covered the traps and chains with dead leaves. Above each trap, he placed a bait of rabbit flesh or a fish head. Standing in the icy stream, he worked a long time at each set until he was proud of the naturalness of its appearance. He'd show Rainbow, he thought, that you didn't need a *wyakin* to catch a wolverine! Then he hurried back to the fire in his lodge to warm the feeling back into his numb and clammy feet.

That afternoon Nat watched for the return of Rainbow eagerly, then anxiously, for the sunny weather had changed. The sky sagged with dull clouds. But the rain he expected did not fall. Instead wind came. Darkness did not bring the Indian boy. Nat could not eat his own supper that night, for thinking of Rainbow who had eaten nothing for two days and who crouched alone somewhere in the black, wind-tossed woods.

He lay down by the lodge fire; watched it die to coals

and then to ashes. The men around him slept but Nat still listened to the roar of the wind in the trees. Now it was growing less.

Then it seemed he was on his way to the sets he had made for the wolverine. So perfectly hidden were his traps that he stepped in one of them. The trap had grown immensely. It clamped both of his feet so tightly he could not feel them. No one would know where he was, he thought, until Rainbow's return. Which might be not at all! Then the skunk-bear came.

It was wide and squat, with two tawny stripes in its brown fur, something like the white stripes of a skunk, and with a plumed tail. But it was taller than the grizzly that had killed Brent's horse. It came slowly, grinning at Nat even while he raised the rifle he was carrying. Why it was a rifle instead of his horn bow he didn't know. He'd have more confidence if it were the bow and he thought of going home to get it, but then, of course, the trap wouldn't let him. So he pulled the trigger.

Its boom was like that of a cannon. It shook the ground Nat lay on and woke him. He was panting. It woke all the men in the lodge with him.

"Queer fer it to thunder in winter!" he heard Brent mutter.

"*Oui*—yes," said Laramie. "But not so strange here as it would be on de plains or mountains."

Bluish light flickered through the smoke-hole and again thunder crashed. Shreds of rain came down and caused some of the men to move their beds. They could hear rain beat against the tule mats of the lodge in sheets. Brent spoke again, voicing what Nat was intensely thinking.

"Rough on that little shaver, alone up in the mountains!"

The freak electrical storm lasted half an hour. The rain continued until nearly morning. At daylight, Nat saddled his horse, intending to join the search he expected the men of the village to make for Rainbow. He waited, impatiently.

The old man who was the village crier rode his goose-rumped horse around the camp the same as he did every morning, calling for everyone to wake up and give thanks that they had lived through another night. Smoke began to rise from the lodges. Squaws went to the river with their water-bags of tightly woven grass. When the men appeared they went away toward the steelhead fishery. Indignantly, Nat announced that he would start alone in the direction taken by Rainbow. Captain Bonneville would not permit him to do so.

"Laramie says you would be interfering," he told Nat. "Besides, you would be more likely to get lost yourself than find your friend."

After a while, to pass the tedious waiting, Nat went to his wolverine sets. Somehow his dream had destroyed the confidence with which he had set the traps. He was not greatly surprised that he found each of the four baits taken and three of the traps sprung by having been turned upside down.

"Thick-skulled of me not to remember," he said to himself aloud, "that Scare-toe has even better reason to know steeltraps than deadfalls! He's been in one."

When Nat returned to the Indian village, Rainbow was there. He looked a little thinner but no worse for his experience. Nat questioned him eagerly about that experience. Rainbow explained that he could not tell anything until after the ceremony the next evening, at which he would announce his name.

Nat, however, told *his* dream and his effort to catch the wolverine. He laughed about it but Rainbow listened solemnly.

"Will you lend me a rifle until tomorrow?" he asked Nat. "And one of your chief's thin fishing lines? Ours of cedar bark are too coarse."

"If I can borrow them," Nat answered. "The captain hasn't given me a rifle since I lost one in the river. A bow suits me better, anyhow."

Nat asked Brent for his rifle. But Brent was that kind of mountain man who hadn't slept with his rifle beyond his reach for years, no matter *where* he slept—and wouldn't now. Laramie was less rigid in his caution. He obliged. The captain supplied a linen trout line. Nat gave the gun and line to Rainbow, confident he was to be a party to some new adventure but the Indian boy disappeared into his lodge with them and Nat saw no more of him that day.

Nor did he catch even a glimpse of him until noon of the next day. Then, roaming about restlessly, Nat saw the Indian boy coming into the farther side of the village. He was bending under some load that was broad as his own back and reached from his shoulders nearly to his heels. Nat ran toward him.

Soon he saw that Rainbow's buckskin shirt was cut.

131

Blood streaked his face and one of his arms. It dripped from the fingers of one hand. Panting, but with a triumphant grin, he dropped to the ground the thick-furred, brown-and-tawny body of a very large wolverine.

Nat, lifting the animal with considerable effort, saw at once that one toe from the right forefoot was missing.

"*How* did you get him?" Nat almost exploded the question. Rainbow answered calmly.

"I fastened the rifle in the fork of a tree. I aimed it at a bait. Then I tied the fishing line from the bait to the trigger."

"And you killed him right there!" Nat cried. "No, he's warm yet. And how was your arm hurt?"

"The gun only wounded Skunk-Bear," Rainbow explained. "I trailed him long ways. He had hidden under fallen tree. I had not brought the rifle because no more powder or bullets. So," he finished simply, "I killed him with a club."

The people of the village were gathering rapidly. They were examining the big wolverine delightedly and asking for a re-telling of the story of the killing of this crafty enemy. Nat ran to get Captain Bonneville to dress Rainbow's many bites and scratches. On the way, he met Swans-lighting-on-the-water, helping her convalescent husband Tu-eka-kas to walk toward the place of the excitement. That the news of their son's accomplishment had run ahead of him, Nat could tell by the calm pride on their faces.

The boy was thinking out loud without knowing it as he led the way back.

"What did you say?" asked Captain Bonneville.

"Huh? Oh, I was just wondering. Rainbow's idea of letting the wolverine shoot itself—did he get it from his dream, or mine? From his new *wyakin* or his own wits? Pretty smart, anyhow."

That night, Nat and the captain and others of his party were invited to the naming ceremony. It was held in the largest lodge, where a line of twelve fires gleamed. The Indians in the front rows were sitting, those behind them were kneeling and those in the rear standing—until the lodge was filled. But the captain was seated next to Tu-eka-kas and Nat was beside him.

There were several other Indian youngsters who, within the past month, had completed their vigils. These were assembled with Strong Eagle. All wore new clothing of whitened buckskin, embroidered with beads or dyed quills.

Beginning with the first, these now announced their names. The crier repeated each name several times to make sure that all heard it correctly. There was Yoomtis Kunnin or Bear Blanket, He-me-ne Mox-mox or Yellow Wolf and a very pretty girl of about thirteen whose voice was so shy and soft that Nat scarcely heard the name she gave. The crier echoed it, Hal pa-win-mi—Dawn. The audience nodded and made sounds of approval.

Last was the turn of the chief's son. With the memory of the strange and violent winter electrical storm fresh in everyone's mind, the people loudly approved the name he gave:

"Hin-mot Too-yah-lat-kekt"—which means Thunder-rolling-to-higher-mountaintops.

In years to come, white men, who certainly could not

handle such a name, were to call him Nez Perce Joseph. When at last his patient people were forced, by years of injustice done them, into a war against the armies of the United States, Chief Joseph was to win the respect of generals seasoned in the War between the States and by years of Indian fighting. "Greatest Indian general," he was pronounced by these men who could compare him to Black Hawk, Sitting Bull and Crazy Horse. "Greatest Indian chief," he has been called by men who also know his life-long efforts for the welfare of his people.

But it was well that Hin-mot and Nat could know nothing of this—well that they could part as just boys who were good friends, the next morning, when Captain Bonneville and his party continued their journey down the Valley of Winding Waters.

CHAPTER 10

Voyageur

Captain Bonneville and his men were loading their horses to leave the village of Tu-eka-kas. There was not so much stuff to pack now. Trading had been good at both the Nez Perce villages where they had stayed. Much of the goods with which they had struggled over the Snake River Mountains had been exchanged for beaver, otter and marten skins. And this store of fur the captain had entrusted to the keeping of Tu-eka-kas until he should return.

As a result, the traders now had more horses than they needed, so they left a few of them here, too. Nat had difficulty deciding whether to take with him his bay Whitefoot or the chestnut Kosooyeen. Going Alone was now fully recovered from his lameness. Nat chose to take him solely because he was strongest and fastest, for he still liked the little bay the best. He left Whitefoot in the care of Rainbow, whom Nat was having difficulty to learn to call Hin-mot. He didn't often attempt the rest of the long, new name.

Hin-mot was present, of course, to tell Nat good-by. Captain Bonneville made one more effort to trade from the boy the skin of the big wolverine. He offered beads, knives, even a rifle with polished brass studs in its varnished stock. Hin-mot shook his head and his father did not try to influence him to accept the bargain offered. The boy's mother, Swans-lighting-on-the-water, spoke now and said she would make a medicine coat for Hin-mot out of the skin.

Nat thought that was a good idea. Certainly the fur was handsome to look at—and mighty warm!

Swan Woman, as she was more often called, had been kind to Nat throughout his stay among the people of her tribe. She had given him choice food, mended his clothes and, in the evenings while she sewed, had told him and Hin-mot legends of the Nez Perces. Many of these, like the stories Nat had heard among the Crows, were adventures and escapades of Coyote. They were whimsical more often than heroic and though some were meant to teach a lesson, it was usually screened by a laugh.

Now, in parting, Swan Woman gave Nat three pairs of moccasins. Two pairs were plain, for everyday wear. The other pair was beautifully beaded, for special occasions.

Nat found but few words to express the thanks he felt, and those few were gruff, for a tightness came to his throat. This glimpse he'd had lately of life inside a kind home was something he hadn't known since Sarah Logan died, except, perhaps, for his stay in the lodge of Swift Bear, chief of the Crows. But there Nat had been a captive, uncertain of what was to be done with him. Far Eagle's kindness and the beginning of their friendship was the main thing he remembered about that. Looking now at the smiling face of Swan Woman made Nat realize that living in a world of men—even ones he admired and liked as much as Brent and Laramie and Captain Bonneville—that sort of a life lacked a good deal.

But the world of men was his world—and before him lay the trail, winding always west!

There was a general handshaking, but Tu-eka-kas made no speech. He said only, "Come back, my brother." The travelers swung up. A few backward looks, a special wave to Hin-mot from Nat—and the Nez Perce village was out of sight.

A man on foot was waiting beside the trail. Though the day was chilly and raw, he wore only a breech-clout, worn moccasins and a ragged red blanket. The blanket had a familiar look—so did the fellow's moonface, though his grin drooped sheepishly.

"Wookawkaw!" Nat cried. "Where have you been? Where's your new shirt and blanket? Or your old shirt and leggins, your bow and knife and hatchet? What's happened to you?"

Woodpecker shrugged sadly. "I have many cousins," he explained. "And they are poor. I can never keep better things than they have. One asks me for my shirt, one for my knife . . ." He spread his empty hands.

Captain Bonneville spoke sternly. "You've been gambling," he said. "Lost even your britches at *lopmix*, the hand game!" The guess was good. Wookawkaw hung his head.

137

Nat had seen much gambling among the Indians—and the mountain men as well. Mostly it was betting on horse races, on shooting matches, on tests of strength. The Nez Perces were addicted to *lopmix,* a version of the pea-and-shell game of white men. The players, in opposing pairs or in teams, faced each other on their knees. They moved their hands, palms down, from side to side and jerked their bodies and chanted in time to a drum. One player held a bit of wood or bone. Deftly he moved it from hand to hand or to the hands of his teammates. The opposing players bet that a certain one of their number could pick the hand in which the object, at that moment, was being held.

Nat had never learned the fascination with which chance grips many persons. To him, it had seemed strange that this simple game, and the fever of the betting, could hold groups of Indians from dark until daylight. Enemy warriors had been known to enter a camp, stand for a time unrecognized among the watchers of the hand game and go away—with the best horses of the village! There were tales of Indians who, with nothing else left, had even bet their scalps.

"I will be your guide again," Wookawkaw offered hopefully. "No one knows the Blue Range better than I. I will kill deer for you—"

"With what?" The captain was not at all pleased that the valuable and well-earned presents he had given Wookawkaw—and the fellow's weapons as well—should have slipped through his fingers so quickly.

"You can lend me a rifle," said Wookawkaw with growing confidence. "And maybe a horse till I meet some of my cousins who can let me have one." His grin was thawing Captain Bonneville's vexation.

"I'll lend you the horse and rifle," he said, "provided you *keep clear* of your cousins! Catch the sorrel, yonder." The captain pointed to one of three extra horses. "But I'll not offer you any clothes. Maybe it will do you good to shiver a little more."

But shivering bodily could not chill the spirits of Wookawkaw, now that he was accepted by his friends again. Even though the captain remained stern toward him and Brent aloof and Tarno sneering, he told his jokes and cut his capers for the benefit of Nat and Laramie. His hunting *was* successful, providing meat for the camps and raw deerskins for himself, out of which he made leggins and a poncho sort of shirt.

He did know the route and he chose good camping spots as well. So they passed through the Blue Range safely, although the snow was deep and the going was hard. Then they crossed treeless plains and followed a small river to its junction with a mighty one. It was a river bigger than the Missouri. Its water, instead of being muddy, was clear and blue.

"*Skookum Chuck*," (Strong Water) said Wookawkaw in the language of the Chinook Indians, which was used in place of the sign language between the tribes of Oregon. "K'lumby *Chuck*."

"K'lumby?" Nat repeated. And then a long "O-o-oh—!" of understanding. "The Columbia!"

It was the River of the West, at last.

139

The Hudson's Bay post of Fort Walla Walla stood at the junction of the little river and the great one. It was surrounded by a stockade of drift logs, with bastions at two corners to give flanking fire on any enemy who might attempt to scale the wall. Not all tribes could be trusted like the Nez Perces.

Chief Clerk Pambrun, in charge here, received the travelers courteously but with a noticeable reserve. Personally, he was glad of visitors at this lonely place. And officially "The Company" stood always ready to extend hospitality. But in the realm of trade, which was the purpose for which the Company of Gentleman Adventurers Trading into Hudson's Bay existed—and had existed more than a century longer than the government of the United States—Captain Bonneville was a rival. Rivals were discouraged, usually with effect.

So, while M. Pambrun lodged and fed the captain and his party admirably, he would not help them in a business way by selling them so much as a plug of tobacco or a pound of flour. He offered no information. To the captain's questions he made clipped replies.

But finding that nothing turned Captain Bonneville from his purpose to go down the Columbia to Fort Vancouver, western headquarters of The Company, certain advice did come from M. Pambrun. He spoke with a convincing sincerity.

The Indians down-river, he said, were a dangerous lot, degenerated by contact with competing white traders and by whiskey they brought in the ships that came to the mouth of the Columbia from—"many parts of the world." The trader was polite enough, speaking to an American, not to say, "from Boston." Of late, lonely travelers along the river had been robbed and sometimes killed. Since the will of the Hudson's Bay was the only law in Oregon, it would be necessary for The Company to send an expedition from Fort Vancouver, should harm come to Captain Bonneville and his men. The safety of The Company's own agents demanded that violence must not be allowed to increase. Quite aside from Captain Bonneville's welfare, it was cheaper to prevent an attack than to punish the Indians for it after it had occurred.

Trader Pambrun explained that there was an excellent way of avoiding the risk. In a day or two an "express" carrying orders and mail would arrive at Fort Walla Walla, en route to Fort Vancouver. It would consist of two large canoes. There would be room for the captain and his men. For a reasonable sum, he could engage passage and arrive at the Fort easily, safely and in half the time that it would take to go with horses.

"But how will we return?" the captain asked.

M. Pambrun said that travelers from Oregon to the United States took passage on a ship. There were several each year. It was a matter of a six-months' voyage by way of Hawaii, then called the Sandwich Islands, and around Cape Horn to Boston. But finding that this was not at all in the captain's plans, the trader added the information that, not long after the arrival of the express, the spring "brigade" would be setting out from Fort Vancouver, with goods and supplies for upriver trading posts. Again, passage could be arranged. Travel would be slower coming

141

upstream with loaded canoes, but even so, the round trip would be quicker by water than by land.

Captain Bonneville was interested. "How do you know the express will arrive soon? Is it coming from Fort Okanagan, one hundred thirty miles upriver?" he asked.

"By way of Okanagan, yes," M. Pambrun replied evenly. "The express comes yearly from York Factory on Hudson's Bay."

"From Hudson's Bay!" the captain echoed in astonishment. "In winter, across two thousand miles of plains?"

"Oh, no! The route of the express is in the bush, far north of the plains, where our trading posts are and where the woods give shelter from storms. It is at least three thousand miles—traveled by dog teams, mostly; then by canoes, when the head of the Columbia is reached."

Captain Bonneville's words were slowed by amazement. "Three thousand miles of deep snows, mountains, rivers, rapids! And you know within *two months* of when to expect it?"

"Within two days," corrected M. Pambrun, patiently. "It is a matter of pride with the voyageurs. They are seldom more than two days late."

And within two days, the express arrived.

It was almost in awe that Nat looked at the voyageurs. Men who could make such a journey on schedule must be more than flesh and blood. But they looked very human, chanting a song in French to which they kept time with their paddles, as they swung their big canoes in to the landing below Fort Walla Walla. They were not gigantic men, nor men with bulging muscles and faces of iron. They were wind-burnt, sinewy men, but around their dark eyes—most of them showing the faint slant of Indian blood—were the crow's-feet lines of ready laughter and of peering into storms and the welter of rapids and the blaze of sun on water. Knot a bright sash around Laramie's waist and a red *fillet* around his head to keep perspiration from his eyes, and he would be one of them. He *was* one of them, except that years ago he had left canoes for horses. He threw his arms around the voyageurs as if they were brothers. His influence may have had something to do with Captain Bonneville's decision to take passage with the express.

There was the question of what to do with their horses. Most of them the captain would have been willing to sell, and take the chance of buying others on his return. But certainly he did not want to dispose of his White Thunder, nor did Nat want to lose Kosooyeen. While for Laramie to sell his Paloos or for Brent to part with Kiowa was unthinkable.

Wookawkaw offered to stay here and take care of the horses and such trade goods as remained in the packs.

It was an idea. But. . . .

Suppose Wookawkaw, heady with the temporary possession of four fast horses, started racing against other Indians. Customary stakes were high. And somewhere among the Yakimas, Paloos and Cayuses who came to trade at Fort Walla Walla there *might* be a horse that could beat even these splendid buffalo runners, especially if their rider were not adept. Or suppose the fever of *lopmix* again got hold of Wookawkaw!

Tarno offered a solution. "This man ain't hankerin' fer no five-hunnerd-mile canoe ride," he said. "I'll stay here at Wally Wally an *help* Woodpecker take keer o' the hosses. *And* he'd better not start any shenanigans."

The arrangement didn't sound pleasant, but the captain believed he could rely on it. And it would save some on passage money. It was finally decided upon. Wookawkaw heard it with a wooden face.

Nat didn't like it, but then Nat didn't like Tarno. He believed Wookawkaw, however reckless he was with his own property, would prove trustworthy with that of some-one else—more so when alone, on his honor, than under the supervision of the scornful Tarno. But Nat's opinion wasn't asked.

The express left the next morning before dawn. Lara-mie plied a paddle and joined with the voyageurs in sing-ing *chansons* of the France none of them had seen.

"It takes *somethin'*," muttered Brent, "to sing before daylight!" The canoes sped down the broad river that seemed still asleep between its dark hills.

Sunlight touched those hills, then the still water. Blue campfire smoke rose at rare intervals along the shore. The measured, silent lift and dip of the paddles was ceaseless. Geese rose honking from a sandbar. A steelhead flashed in a curving jump.

The canoes were big and beamy. Nat could see no seams in them, yet he could not believe that trees grew anywhere that were big enough to be hollowed into canoes of this size. When he felt sufficiently acquainted with 'Poleon, the steersman, he asked him where and how such canoes were made.

"*Oui*," said 'Poleon, "dere's plentee tree along coast to mak' bigger canoe as dis. Don' tak' so big a log as she looks. Klatsop canoe-makers shape de log on outside, den hollow it from a narrow cut along top. Put some water in it. Den hunnerds of red-hot stones. Cover wit' blankets. W'en she's steamed good, dey call up whole village. Ev'ry body pull on gunwales an' spread de canoe out, wide. Put in thwarts to hold it. Fasten de high, carved pieces on bow an' stern. See, she's steady. Injuns up coast mak' war-canoes to carry fifty men out of one cedar log. Go long ways on Salt Chuck—dat's ocean—in such canoes. Jus' sam'," he added "*la bon pirogue*—de good canoe—she's birch bark. Fast. Light. Easy carry. Easy fix!"

The voyageurs paddled three hours then stopped for breakfast. Four hours more and they put ashore for a hasty lunch. Another seven and they chose their landing and made camp in the dark. This they continued day after day, rain or shine.

But at the twenty-foot drop of Celilo Falls, where dozens of fishing platforms were ingeniously built above the cascading water, they landed to portage. Here was the Indian village of Wishram. And here Low-loo-can, *tyee* —chief—of the Chinooks, stood ready to collect a tax for permitting the canoes to be carried across his land. He was backed by a number of his tribesmen. Nat stared at them all in blank surprise.

He realized that perhaps the fact that the Indians of this region spent most of their lives sitting in canoes or hunched on fishing platforms had something to do with their squat build. But they seemed to him—and were—of a different racial stock from the lithe, erect horsemen he knew. Their features were broad and, to Nat, were not beautified by the bands of red or black paint that slanted like big chevrons from the bridge of their flat noses downward across their cheeks.

But the thing about them Nat disapproved of most was that their clothing was that of white men. It had been worn out when they received it, no telling how long ago, but had probably been given to them in pretense of an honor. Low-loo-can, as befitted the *tyee*, wore an epauletted coat that had once glorified a naval officer. On his coarse, unbraided hair was a civilian gentleman's high beaver hat. The coat had been slept in many times and the hat was crumpled to a rakish tilt. All the Indians smelled fearfully of fish.

'Poleon, who was *bourgeois*, or leader, of the express, offered Low-loo-can the customary two blankets, one for each canoe, for in the country of the Columbia, the blanket, as Nat had already learned, was the unit of value instead of the beaver "plew." For years the "Great Company," the Hudson's Bay, had humored this petty *tyee* by paying him this tribute.

But now Low-loo-can shook his head and gutturaled in Chinook. *"Wake mika kla-ta-wah kopa hui-hut. Potlatch nika ikt-lakit blanket."* (You will not cross the portage unless you pay me six blankets.) 'Poleon's black eyebrows bounced.

VOYAGEUR

"Hi-yu kultis wah-wah! Halo nika potlatch!" (Much worthless talk! I'll not give!) he thundered back.

But Low-loo-can scowled and repeated his demand. The number of Chinooks behind him increased and most of them were carrying guns.

"Let me pay him," said Captain Bonneville.

"No!" roared 'Poleon. "Pay him six blankets dis tam—nex' tam he want *twelve. Him* try to hold up De Company!" It was an atrocious crime in 'Poleon's eyes. No one understood the necessity of firmness, in its place, better than Captain Bonneville and he said no more.

As for their own safety, it seemed ridiculous for men who had dared the proud, fierce Crows and Blackfeet to be alarmed at such sorry looking Indians as these. 'Poleon waved them back and told his men to pick up one of the canoes. The big dugout was heavy and Laramie, who throughout the voyage had served as one of the crew, helped to shoulder it. Captain Bonneville assigned Brent to remain as guard of the other canoe and the packs of Company orders, mail and special supplies. That left only the Captain and Nat to escort the men carrying the canoe. 'Poleon offered the boy his smooth-bore musket but Nat declined it and strung his bow. This was one of the times when Nat believed a bow was superior to a gun because range did not matter and a good bowman could shoot four or five times while a muzzle-loader was being reloaded.

The captain's rifle was thrown casually across his left arm but his right thumb and forefinger were ready on hammer and trigger. He did not threaten but he alertly faced the twenty scowling Indians. What they would dare to attempt could not be predicted by anything he had learned of Indians of the plains.

The voyageurs each had both hands busy holding the upturned canoe on their shoulders. Their eyes must watch their footing on the rough and slippery trail. The great river thundered down its cascade on one side of them. On the other side was a dense growth of brush.

Nat flanked the canoe. He wished he had eyes all around his head. The eyes he did have studied the brush where more Indians might be lurking. Occasionally he glanced back toward Captain Bonneville.

The threatening Chinooks were following closely and to keep his front to them meant that most of the captain's steps were taken backward. Nat saw an Indian *behind* the captain rise to a crouch in the bushes beside the trail.

He was unarmed, or Nat would have shot him. Nat called, but the boom of the falls drowned his voice. Before he could guess the Indian's intention, the fellow lunged forward with a forked pole that had lain beside him. The fork caught the captain's knees from behind and they buckled under him. He fell on the sloping, rocky ground.

Knife drawn, Low-loo-can sprang forward. His surly crew was at his heels.

Nat's bow twanged; the sound low but more commanding than a snake's hiss. His mark was irresistible. Ever since he had seen that rakish top hat he had itched to put an arrow through it. Now he did.

The arrow snapped the hat off Low-loo-can's head. It astonished him and it stopped him flat with its forceful warning. The rest of the Indians checked their rush, also.

Had Nat killed their chief, they would have surged forward in reckless fury. The boy whipped another arrow from the quiver on his shoulder and faced them, bow drawn. They knew now how straight and fast he could shoot. The guns of the Chinooks remained uncertainly half-raised.

The instant he was on his knees, Captain Bonneville had swung his rifle. His blow knocked senseless the Indian who had upset him. With Nat beside him, the captain herded the Chinooks back to their squalid village. The voyageurs completed the portage.

The express sped on down the big river. On the bow-piece of one of the canoes, carved as the head of a huge frog, Laramie had pegged a tall, battered beaver hat.

CHAPTER 11

Fort

The voyageurs portaged The Dalles, where the River of the West split into three channels and plunged through parallel chasms slashed through strange layers of lava rock. The canoes sped on. The bare hills along the river became timbered and grew into bold bluffs. But far above these humped ridges towered two snowy peaks—one on either side of the river—symmetrical as giant tepees. Nat saw them rose-pink in the dawn, cloud-draped at midday, silver under the moon. Captain George Vancouver, the British explorer, had named them Mt. Hood and Mt. St. Helens. Nat was more interested in the voyageurs' fancy that they were the lodgepoles that upheld the sky.

There was one more portage, The Cascades. It was in a range of mountains named for the rapids they caused in the river, where it had cut its way through their great ridges of folded rock. The next day, toward evening, the canoes swept up to the landing below the western headquarters of the Hudson's Bay Company, Fort Vancouver.

FORT

The fort, surrounded by its high stockade of pointed logs, stood on a plain on the north bank of the river. Around it were wide fields. In meadows nearer the river grazed herds of horses and cattle and flocks of sheep. A street, lined on either side with the neat log cabins of Company *engages*, led from the gates of the fort to the riverbank.

Someone had seen the express far up the river and a crowd had gathered at the low, wooden dock. Canadians welcomed their fellow voyageurs with whoops and bear hugs. Indian wives presented some of the canoemen with solemn-eyed sons or daughters in beaded black velvet papoose slings. They had arrived since the fathers left for York Factory, the summer before. Pretty young women blushed to publicly welcome boisterous sweethearts. Children of all sizes packed close among their elders.

These were English and Scottish clerks and traders, burly Scottish farmers and blacksmiths, Canadian bakers, the tailor, the flour miller and grizzled voyageurs who had spent their share of sixteen-hour days on paddle and tumpline and were now Company pensioners. There were also brown men whom Nat thought to be another sort of Indian, new to him. They were striking because of their huge size, their ready smiles and because their black hair was fine and slightly kinky, instead of being coarse and straight, like that of all Indians the white boy had seen.

Then he heard the words *"le Doctaire"* repeated by many lips. The noise stilled. Looking in the direction in which all other eyes turned, Nat saw a man who was a head taller even than Brent coming down the street from the gate of the stockade. He was erect, deep-chested, and he moved with swinging strides. His ruddy face was smooth-shaven but his hair was worn at the usual shoulder length. It was a mane of pure white—prematurely so, Nat guessed correctly, for in all other respects he had the appearance of a vigorous middle age. The crowd made way for him, not fearfully but with a glad respect.

Nat knew him; knew him well by all that he had heard Laramie and the voyageurs tell. He was Doctor John McLaughlin, chief factor of the western department of the Hudson's Bay Company. He ruled an empire extending from the Rocky Mountains to the Pacific Coast and from the Spanish territory of California to Russian America, just beginning to be called Alaska then—ruled it with a mingling of kindness, firmness and justice that is seldom found in men given complete power.

Like the strange mixture of men he governed, McLaughlin was himself a mixture of Irish, Scotch and French-Canadian stock, while his wife, like Laramie, was half Ojibway. By study in Montreal and Paris he had become a doctor of medicine, then entered the service of the Northwest Fur Company at Grande Portage, on the Great Lakes. When the "Nor'westers," the Canadian company which had established most of the trading posts west of the Rockies, united with its deadly rival, the British Hudson's Bay Company, under the older company's name, McLaughlin had risen rapidly in a system where promotion was traditionally slow.

He dealt with the Indians fairly. He limited or forbade the use of liquor in trade. Among his host of subordinate officers and employees he was doctor, counselor and friend. Even among those who had completed their service with the Company and settled on farms in this Oregon they had grown to love, he enforced honesty, sobriety and—what was sometimes harder—industry.

In one day he might arrange with the pompous Governor of California for the exportation of cattle to Oregon, then deal with the chief of a dozen Klatsop fishermen for the season's price of dried salmon, and then negotiate with the Czar's appointed head of the Russian-American Company for trading rights on the Skeena or Stikeen rivers, a thousand miles to the north. In all cases and at all times he was the shrewd and vigorous manager of The Company—The Hudson's Bay.

As Nat had listened to all this being told and re-told on the down-river voyage, he had made a wide allowance for French-Canadian fervor and extravagance. But he threw that allowance overboard when the huge man with the twinkling gray eyes, so deep-set under bushy brows, shook his hand. Surely it was without condescension and with as much heartiness as he displayed when he shook the hand of 'Poleon, his trusty *bourgeois*, or of Captain Bonneville. And that was *before* he inquired the meaning of the top hat crowning the big frog's head on the bow of the canoe.

'Poleon told the story of Low-loo-can and his unruly Chinooks—told it with both indignation and humor. The Chief Factor's laugh boomed.

"Trust a lad," he said, "to do the right thing at the right time!" And he gave Nat an approving pat on the back—which nearly knocked the breath out of him.

153

Dr. McLaughlin took Captain Bonneville to his own house. Laramie, who would have been at home with any of the *engages*, recognized among those now stationed at the fort one called Etienne Boulain, an older companion of many trails in former years. He and Brent were made doubly welcome in Etienne's home. Nat would rather have accompanied them, but, as orderly to Captain Bonneville, he went where the captain went.

The Chief Factor's big house was in the center of the area enclosed by the stockade. Two ship's cannon were mounted on its broad steps, with a neat pyramid of cannon-balls beside each. Nat's interest in them brought from Dr. McLaughlin another laugh.

"Stick to your bow, my lad," he advised. "Those cannon have never been fired, nor will they be so long as they stay here. This is not a dangerous region, like that around Fort Walla Walla. Vancouver is a fort in name alone."

However, the Company's offices, warehouses and shops were all within the stockade. Even as he hurried past them Nat was impressed with their orderliness and the beautiful shrubs, grass and flowers of the grounds.

At sundown he heard the ringing of a deep-toned bell. It was housed under a little roof on the top of a tall post. All work stopped—the sorting and baling of fur in the warehouses, the slow turning of the stone burrs of the flour mill. The fires went out in the forges, the men trooped from the fields.

A clerk hauled down from its tall flagpole the British Union Jack . . . and from a pole of equal height beside it the flag with the two beaver supporting a shield and the

initials, H.B.C. Laramie had laughingly told Nat the
letters meant "Here Before Christ," and from the look of
order and permanence so stamped upon this place, compared to the brief and rowdy rendezvous camps of the
American traders, Nat could see the meaning back of Laramie's joke.

An hour later, the bell sounded again and the captain
and Nat accompanied Factor McLaughlin to the dining
hall. It was lighted by more candles than Nat had seen
before in all his life.

All the officers and clerks at this post of the Company
were present and the long table was filled. The men wore
cloth coats and cravats, they were shaven and their hair was
neatly combed. Nat and the captain had been loaned coats
of suitable size and Nat did not know whether he was more
uncomfortable in someone else's coat of a style he had never
seen before than he would have been in his out-of-place
buckskin shirt. There was a white cloth on the table and
an array of gleaming silver beside his plate that frightened
Nat. It had been a year since he had sat upon even a bench,
let alone a polished chair, and put his feet under a table—
or eaten with a fork! Besides, in all his life, he had only
eaten with a steel or pewter one. Now he *did* wish he was
with Brent and Laramie, among the half-Indian youngsters
in the Canadian's cabin!

Still, there was a strong curiosity in Nat and a thirst for
new experiences. This promised to be one, sure enough—
after the way mountain men cooked their meat on sticks
and ate it with their hunting knives.

The men around Nat remained standing until the doctor

took his place at the head of the table. Still standing, they lifted their glasses together, said "To the King!" and drank their wine. Belatedly, Nat tasted his and didn't like it. He felt better when he remembered seeing only water in Dr. McLaughlin's glass.

Then the waiters served roast ducks, roast beef, vegetables, bread—Nat hadn't tasted it for months—jellies, and cooked fruits, a pudding, strong black tea. The food was excellent, Nat thought, but he missed the wild flavor from all but the ducks—and the smoke seasoning. Only the tea was the same as by a campfire. No, even tea tasted better from a buffalo horn than from a white cup so thin Nat was afraid it would break at his touch.

Also, he could not taste keenly because he was too busy seeing and hearing what went on around him, although he could have understood more of a conversation in Crow or Nez Perce than he got from the quick-spoken words of the Englishmen or the burry pronunciation of the men from Scotland and the Orkney Islands.

Then, as the meal finished, Nat was choked by embarrassment when Doctor McLaughlin called the attention of the whole assembly to him by asking Captain Bonneville to relate the incident at Celilo Falls. Everyone applauded when the captain finished telling how Nat had prevented robbery and bloodshed by skillfully shooting Low-loo-can through his absurd dignity rather than his greedy heart.

Though wine was on the table, no one drank of it heavily. Nor did anyone appear to eat half the quantity that was consumed at a feast by Indians or mountain men. The diners rose together and went into another room to smoke and talk. Some of the clerks who were still in their teens gathered around Nat and asked him many questions about the Indians beyond the mountains, of hunting buffalo and how he had learned to shoot so well with a bow.

In turn, they told him of their voyage from London to the Columbia River—of the stormy rounding of Cape Horn and the warm, dreamy beauty of the Hawaiian Islands, where all ships in the Pacific stopped for fresh water and supplies. Nat, who had never seen wider water than the Columbia as it flowed by Fort Vancouver, had as much difficulty in imagining an ocean that it took months to sail across as these young men did in picturing a herd of buffalo one could not see beyond. From them Nat learned that the huge brown men he had seen at the landing were not Indians but Kanakas, Hawaiian Islanders, hired by the Hudson's Bay Company. When Nat returned to their room with Captain Bonneville, he was warmed with the feeling of having had a pleasant evening, after all.

"But why do they make all that fuss about their supper?" he asked. The captain considered his words before he replied.

"Nat," he said, "you've lived always on the frontier where life changes so frequently that few customs are formed—and no traditions at all. The mountain men, in particular, have been a poor example to you in the niceties of living, for though they are brave and loyal, they have sluffed off all the polite customs of their own race and adopted few of the courteous ways of the Indians they live among. To you, as to them, eating is to satisfy hunger, nothing more.

157

"But in older countries, where people have lived for many generations, customs develop that have a deep place in their lives. For instance, to take one's place at the table before all are ready is to appear greedy. To rise before the rest have finished shows that one is again thinking only of himself. To observe these and many other polite manners, to have the table attractive and the food well served, becomes a standard by which such people judge the way they live.

"So Doctor McLaughlin," the captain continued, "insists that the officers and the men who may become officers in this company eat together in the manner of the gentlemen in the land from which they came. It keeps them from becoming careless in their other habits of life. In the army, we do the same, so far as is possible, and call the result 'morale.' "

Nat thought a moment. Finally he declared, "Maybe something like that is behind many of the customs of the Indians. Like, in a Crow tepee, it is said to 'break friendship' if you pass between a seated person and the fire. I guess that's because if you do it, you shut him off from the light and warmth."

"Exactly," agreed Captain Bonneville. "We are wrong when we class as superstitions the customs of any people we do not take the trouble to understand."

Nat climbed into bed, but that brief reference to the Crows had set him thinking—thinking of Far Eagle . . . and the brown horse, Pierre. And those troubled thoughts, more than the uncomfortable softness of the first bed he had tried to sleep in for a year, kept him awake for a long time. When the big bell waked Captain Bonneville at day-light, he found Nat rolled up in a blanket and sleeping on the floor.

That day the captain and his party were shown the many industries of Fort Vancouver. Here, in the forges, farm machinery was repaired and at least forty hatchets a day were made for the Indian trade. In the dairy, butter and cheese were made, not only for the many people who lived at the Fort but for those at outlying posts where agriculture could not be carried on. Flour was milled for Company needs and for export to Alaska. At a small stream nearby, a water wheel ran a busy little sawmill. Wool was carded and spun, beef prepared for shipment to other trading posts.

As Nat rode with Brent across the seven hundred acres of rich, flat fields, he watched sharply the light that glowed in his friend's usually calm and rather lonely eyes. Brent didn't need to say, "What a long, straight furrow a man can plow here!" for a jealous resentment to burn in Nat. What business had Brent with furrows? Why, he was the best beaver trapper, the best buffalo hunter, the best scout —between the Snake River and Santa Fe! Trouble was, Nat remembered, Brent wasn't now between the Snake River and Santa Fe. They shouldn't have left the moun-tains, the beaver and buffalo land!

The next day Nat went with Brent and Laramie and Laramie's old friend, Etienne Boulain. They crossed the Columbia and paddled some distance up the Wilamette River, which here entered the great river from the south. They were bound for the settlement at French Prairie where many retired *engages* of The Company—other of

159

Laramie's old friends among them— had taken land. With the men in the canoe was Etienne's daughter, Angelique.

She was one of the young women Nat had noticed at the dock when the express arrived—one that would keep a person from remembering very much about the rest! But one that had *not* welcomed a sweetheart among the returning voyageurs. She handled a paddle with a graceful strength and as much skill as her father or Laramie—much more than Brent or Nat. It was explained that she was going with them to visit girl friends at the settlement but Nat guessed that Laramie had more to do with her presence among them than anyone else. Laramie talked and joked with her constantly. The girl's bell-like laughter made Nat, who was in the bow, turn so frequently he grew angry at himself for doing so. But he continued to look at her often and noted that the eyes of Brent, who sat behind her, were also fixed on her thoughtfully. Angelique was drawing too much attention and Nat wished she'd stayed at home.

Fertile farms, comfortable cabins, great log barns and big families were the rule in French Prairie. People who anchored themselves to the ground, Nat supposed, thought these things satisfying. A warm welcome was given to Laramie and all who had come with him. Food in abundance was set before them. The air buzzed with talk. A dance was arranged, to be held that evening at the home of the settler with the largest house.

A horse race was held that afternoon. Some of the Canadians worked up a lot of excitement over it. In Nat it aroused only a mild interest. He was sure that at least four of the horses they had left with Wookawkaw—White Thunder, Kosooyeen, the Paloos and particularly the big pinto, Kiowa—could have beaten the winner after spotting him a start of a dozen lengths. He also thought the riders didn't show half the skill of Indians. And the bets, for all the excitement, were in sums of less value than a beaver plew. Would they have the nerve to race where the rule was, "Winner takes the loser's horse"?

Sundown came, and the still evening air carried the lowing of cows, coming placidly in to be milked, the bleating of sheep and the barking of dogs that drove the silly, helpless animals to their pens. Smoke hung in the moist air; chimney smoke! The air didn't stretch your lungs like mountain air and the smoke lacked the tang of campfire smoke. A snipe, making a strange, winnowing sound as it poised in the air above a meadow, was all that Nat could see or hear that interested him sharply. He wondered, a little, what had taken the edge off things.

That night he stood in a crowded corner of the St. Anns home while fiddles scraped and couples, old and young, danced with gusto and huge enjoyment. But none of it rubbed off on Nat.

Laramie's first partner was Angelique. Of course! Nat didn't have to know anything about dancing to know that they were the most graceful and looked the best together of all the couples on the floor. Suppose—the thought gouged its way roughly through the boy's mind—suppose his good friend Laramie decided to *stay* here among these land-bound folk? Didn't go back to the mountains at all!

The music stopped. Partners were changed. The next

161

dance began and Nat stiffened and his jaw dropped, for Brent Logan—Nat's sensible, stoical mountain man—was dancing with pretty Angelique Boulain!

He *could* dance, too. Brent and Angelique also made a pair that were followed by many eyes. Nat had the queerest mixture of feelings! He was proud of Brent, and at the same time it was as though he'd just caught his friend stealing horses . . . or in something almost that far from the idea he'd always had of Brent.

Other young men danced with Angelique. Most often it was Laramie. Brent danced with other girls, and with their Indian mothers, too, as the company warmed with their fun. But every now and then he managed to claim Angelique. These social capers of both his friends made Nat feel totally left out—and determined to stay out, too!

Since it gave him nettle stings to look at Angelique, whether she danced with Brent or with Laramie, Nat watched a much younger girl who wore a blue ribbon in her hair. He noticed that, although her hair was dark, as was that of all the girls, it was not black like theirs. Some ways the light struck it filled it with coppery gleams. Otherwise, she looked much like the Nez Perce girl in the naming ceremony, the one called Hal-pa-win-mi—Dawn. Nat wished he were back in Hin-mot's lodge . . . or in the lodge of Far Eagle, the Crow.

Of course, when the girl looked at Nat, he looked at someone else.

The manager of the dance called, *"Au choix des femmes!"* The girls were picking their partners this time. How, Nat wondered—and why—did a girl put so much

162

mischief in her eyes as was in those of Angelique as she led Laramie toward the center of the room? She had Laramie hooked. No need to be tricky about it!

A hand touched Nat's arm lightly. He turned—and gave a start. The girl with the blue ribbon was smiling up at him, smiling with her lips and with her eyes. Nat was surprised that her eyes were not black, either, like those of the other girls. They were a clear, light brown that made him think of the water in a woodland creek when the sun strikes through to the bottom and picks out flecks of gold where the current is stirring the sand. Then he heard her voice and knew with a jolt that she was asking *him* to dance.

Finally he found his tongue. "I don't—don't know how," he stammered. He felt hot and cold at the same time and was hatefully conscious of the amused eyes that were on him.

"Please dance, Meestair Nat." The girl tugged lightly on the fringes of his buckskin shirt. But Nat was certain that even the pinto, Kiowa, couldn't have pulled him out on the dance floor, where he'd be helpless as an unshod horse on ice. He shook her off roughly and backed deeper into his corner. The girl tossed her head like a pretty filly and went to an overgrown boy a year or so older than Nat, who fairly jumped to meet her. He danced like a landslide, Nat thought. Angry at the girl for making him feel foolish, at the boy for being able to do anything *he* couldn't, at everyone who had laughed, and most of all at himself, Nat went out of the house.

The night air soon chilled him but it did not drive him

163

back inside. He went to the barn. There he found a horse blanket and with it crawled into the haymow. The smell of horses was familiar and good. Although the smell of cows that came with it was a stench, Nat finally went to sleep.

Outside, the sun was shining when Brent found and woke him. "You cheated yourself out of a right fine midnight supper," Brent said. "And a lot of fun. But I reckon you'd have shined in the dance if you'd known how. We're stayin' here a few days, so you've a prime chance to learn."

Nat's reply was a grunt. But hot food and the good spirits of the Canadians at the breakfast table improved his mood. No one so much as mentioned that Nat had been at the dance. Even Cecille St. Anns—she of the blue hair ribbon—had a smile for him that did not seem to go back of the present moment, as she served him a second helping of bacon and hot biscuits. Nat was ashamed of his rudeness of last night.

He cleared his throat and spoke to her, apart from the lively table talk. "I can show you how to shoot a bow, or talk with your hands, or—or call a squirrel down from a tree."

She laughed. "I theenk I like to talk to *cheval*—to horse," she replied. "Ees it true, as La Ramie says, that Eendians call you 'He who talks to a horse?' I like La Ramie, don't you? Do you theenk he will take Angelique for hees wife and leeve at French Prairie? I hope yes, don't you?"

Before Nat could decide where to begin an answer to that, Cecille's mother called her to bring the empty dishes

164

from the table. The men had risen and were filing out of the house. M. St. Anns supplied horses and Brent, Laramie and Nat, with Etienne and several more of Laramie's old friends, went to visit neighboring farms, prosperous in a simple pioneer way. Then they rode on to look at several promising pieces of raw land. Nat was sure Laramie was being urged by his friends to give up his roving life with its dangers and settle here among his kind. Nat resented their influence mightily, though he felt it was small beside that of Angelique. He watched narrowly as Brent silently considered the land.

They stayed four days at French Prairie and the hospitality of the Canadians showed no sign of wearing thin. A dance was held each night. Laramie insisted on teaching Nat how to take part, but found out soon that he could turn most of the instruction over to Cecille. And Nat found that no one was laughing at his inability. As soon as he could laugh at his own awkwardness he got rid of most of it. He learned that there was pleasure in moving to music that he hadn't guessed. By the last evening, he was able to dance four dances with Cecille without stepping on her moccasined feet more than twice.

He also found a chance to show her a little of his skill with horses. There were none here that he knew, but he proved how quickly he could make one of them like him. Nat and Cecille went for a ride. He could tell at once that she had never been on a horse before.

That struck Nat with a shock. But such helplessness was the result, he decided, of living in a house that stayed still. People who lived in tepees began riding horses while they

165

were still in papoose slings and learned to ride without ever knowing when.

But if Cecille was scared, she didn't show it. Nat hesitated to exhibit his skill, thinking he might make her feel somewhat as he had felt that first night at the dance. But she urged him on until finally he was riding in a big circle at full speed, hanging on the side of the horse by one arm and one leg and shooting his bow at a stump, rapidly and with some accuracy, from under the horse's neck.

Cecille, however, showed Nat how to catch trout in a small stream that crossed her father's land. She used a willow pole, a strong thread and a bent pin on which small, bright feathers had been tied. Skillfully she landed six rainbows—while four were getting away from Nat. Remembering the steelhead, Nat decided he wasn't much of a fisherman.

Suddenly it was the morning when Nat and the rest were to start back to Fort Vancouver. Nat found he was no longer in a hurry to go. But they must. The upriver brigade wouldn't wait.

A crowd went with them to the canoe landing. Nat walked beside Cecille and couldn't think of a word to say.

"I like you, Nat," she said when it was time for him to take his place in the canoe. "Come back."

Nat knew it would be easy to promise. But he had been thinking very soberly that the Crow country, to which he was going, was a long, long way off. "I don't know," he said with that honesty which can also be unkind. "Goodby."

166

FORT

Half of the way back to Fort Vancouver Nat was wondering why there was a chill in Cecille's "Good-by." The remaining half of the way he was still wondering—why he couldn't have said, "I want to come back. I will if I can."

CHAPTER 12

Kiowa

They were crossing the Columbia to the Fort.

"Look!" cried Angelique. All eyes turned in the direction in which she pointed, downstream.

Against a setting sun stood tall masts and wide yardarms, spread with more canvas than Nat had supposed there was in the whole world. A ship many times bigger than Nat's imaginings came up the river on the sea wind. She anchored abreast the dock.

"The *Nereid*," Etienne said. "The Company ship. She come from London each year."

That night, Captain Royale and three of his officers from the *Nereid* were guests at Dr. McLaughlin's table. The next morning Captain Bonneville and Nat went aboard the ship. The boy explored her from bow to stern. He even climbed into her rigging, higher than her sailors expected to see any landlubber climb. Mountain cliffs had cured Nat of a fear of height. But it was beyond him to understand how men could work up there, setting or reefing

168

sails, when wind and rain tore at them and the ship rolled, as he could vaguely imagine she must.

The visit to the ship was a thrilling experience to Nat but it gave him no desire to go to sea. He'd take his chances with Indians and buffalo. He was glad the brigade was to start upriver the next day.

In some ways, his haste to start back puzzled Nat a little. He had followed the long trail west for nearly a year with such burning eagerness. But now he had reached the place where there was no more "west" ahead of him. He found that the free, adventurous life he had just learned to live was fitted again into a safe, regulated pattern. It seemed that he had overshot his mark.

Nat knew that Captain Bonneville was eager to start back, with a clearer reason. It was urgent that he get back to Horse Prairie and rejoin his trappers. But while here the captain had been learning all he could of the methods and opportunities of the fur trade on the Pacific Coast.

"Plainly Dr. McLaughlin is not trying to conceal anything from me," he said to Nat. The captain had a way, when they were alone, of discussing many subjects on which Nat might or might not feel able to offer an opinion of his own. "Not once," the captain continued, "has there been a chill in the doctor's hospitality. I think he is taking this way of convincing me that his company has the trade in such secure monopoly that competition would be financially fatal. Here, near their stronghold, I believe that is true. But back toward the mountains there may still be good openings. To discourage me in that direction, McLaughlin, like Pambrun, will not sell me a shilling's worth of anything I need. He will, however, accept a fat fare for shipping us back upriver, out of his country. He is frank about it and I still respect him and value his friendship."

They were interrupted by a knock. At the door stood Brent and Laramie. There was a pause before either of the mountain men spoke. Nat was certain he knew its meaning. Laramie had come to be relieved of his pledge to complete the year in the employ of Captain Bonneville. Angelique had won the jolly rover from his endless mountain trails, from the wild, free life. Laramie would "settle down."

"I hate to quit you, Cap'n. But I reckon I'll stay here."

Nat had a numbed feeling that made him doubt his ears. Those were the words—almost—that he was listening for, but not in the voice he expected. The voice was *Brent's*.

Nat opened his mouth but nothing came out of it. He heard Captain Bonneville's words, crisp with surprise and disappointment.

"I hate to lose you, Logan, especially to the opposition. Has McLaughlin offered you more pay? I suppose," he added, "you are speaking for the two of you."

Laramie broke in then. *"Morbleu—non!* I am not leaving you. I start back wit' you now. Been here long 'nough!"

Brent, too, spoke emphatically. "And *I* am not goin' to work for the Hudson's Bay! I'm takin' me a farm, over there in French Prairie. At last I'm goin' to plow that long, straight furrow!"

"And Nat?" asked Captain Bonneville.

"I have no blood claim on him," Brent said. "But I'm hopin' he'll stay with us."

170

"Us?" Nat had found his voice.

"Yes," said Brent evenly. "Today Cap'n Royale of the *Nereid* is marryin' me to Angelique Boulain."

Captain Bonneville spoke, but the words came to Nat as though his ears were muffled by a blanket. They were—a blanket of astonishment. And of rising rage at those flashing black eyes of Angelique's.

"Then let me be the first to offer my congratulations," the captain was saying. "You've lost no time! I'll release you, of course. And pay you to date. I wish you both much happiness."

"Thank ye, Cap'n."

Then Brent's voice turned strangely gentle and earnest. "An' you're stayin' with us, Nat? I've spoken to Angelique an' she wants ye."

Slowly Nat shook his head. It would have been hard to hold to that answer if Brent were going to live on his farm alone. But Nat was not staying under the same roof with Angelique! She had stolen Brent from him and she had tricked Laramie to do it, playing one against the other. She was nothing like Brent's former wife, Sarah Logan. It did not occur to Nat that he knew Sarah only through the memory of a small boy to whom Sarah had been kind. He did not know that a woman can be an artful sweetheart but a faithful wife—or that Brent's loneliness might be cured by someone who was not the same as Sarah. Nat knew almost nothing about women. In this sudden situation, he knew almost nothing at all—except that he was *not* going to French Prairie and be an intruder in Brent's new life.

He said this with a shake of his head.

Then a certain thought made him break out quickly. "But you'll be coming with us as far as Fort Walla Walla, to get Kiowa!"

Brent smiled. "Hardly," he said, "on my wedding day. If you're sure you won't stay, Nat, you kin have Kiowa."

Nat only stared and Brent said it again. "Nat, Kiowa's yours. Do what you like with him."

"I'd rather—" Nat started to say in a lonely tone—and bit it off. He straightened and when he spoke again his voice was deeper, older. Brent recognized a firmness in it that made him glad.

"Thanks, Brent," Nat said. "You know Kiowa will always mean a lot to me. The real reason I can't stay here with you is not because I'm cross. It's because I must learn what became of Far Eagle. You know it was to save me that he killed the Indian who proved to be one of his own tribe—his father's friend. And that to try to make it right was the reason he took the risks of going back alone to the Absaroka country. Maybe he's safe. Maybe there's nothing I can do to help him. But maybe *there is*. Anyway, I've got to know what happened to him."

"Then good luck, Nat. An' see ye stay close to Cap'n Bonneville." Brent held Nat's hand a moment in an iron grip. After the captain and Laramie had also shaken Brent's hand, they watched him go out the fort's big gate to the home of Etienne Boulain—and Angelique. For once the voluble Laramie said nothing.

Nat was still puzzling how a laughing voice, soft hair and dancing black eyes could make a man like Brent toss away a horse he had risked his life to steal back from the Crows—the best horse that ever wore hide! Well, not "toss away," exactly. It gave Nat a lift to feel so sure that Brent would neither have given nor sold Kiowa to anyone else.

The brigade of ten long, heavily loaded canoes worked its way up the Columbia. The voyageurs sailed briskly on the sea wind where it funneled through the mountain passes. They paddled tirelessly against the current in the more quiet reaches. Nat, among them, paddled not so tirelessly and with far greater impatience.

The voyageurs *cordelled* the canoes up stretches of swifter water, pulling from shore like draft horses on the long towline while bow-paddler and steersman kept each canoe off the rocks with pole and paddle. And they portaged; the Cascades, the Dalles, Celilo Falls. The crews spent long days at this wearing work, every man carrying in his tumpline a load almost as great as that usually placed upon a pack horse. And then the huge canoes were carried on the shoulders of eight or ten men on the rough trails around each rapids.

At Wishram, the village beside Celilo Falls, Low-loo-can was on hand to collect his tax. He accepted his one blanket per canoe grumpily but without his former demand for a raise in tribute. The *bourgeois* of the brigade, one Jacques Belladeau, gave him back his high hat. At McLaughlin's order, it had been mended, cleaned and blocked by the tailor at Fort Vancouver. But the matter of the hat was still a tender subject to the chief. Even its return in such improved condition did not put him in an amiable mood. He forbade his Chinooks, though offered good pay, to help with the portaging. This delayed the brigade an extra day. And all the days dragged for Nat, so eager was he to reach Fort Walla Walla—and his pinto, Kiowa.

Bend after bend in the big river appeared, slowly approached and passed astern. Then at last the bend revealing the drift-log stockade!

Nat didn't expect his Kiowa to be at the landing to meet him. But he did look for Wookawkaw and Tarno. Neither was there. Captain Bonneville asked about them quickly. The good-natured face of M. Pambrun became suddenly grave.

"*Ah, mon Capitaine,* the news is bad," he said. "Very bad! Your Nez Perce and your white man, Tarno, seem to have quarreled about something. Anyway, Tarno shot the Indian. It is the white man, I am sure, who is the rascal, for he took all your horses and goods and went away. Where?" M. Pambrun shrugged. It was not a gesture of indifference. It was one of questioning and matched the pained expression on his face.

"Wookawkaw shot!" gasped Nat.

"Was the Indian killed?" demanded Captain Bonneville.

"*Nom d'un chien!*—name of a dog! Dat Tarno!" came from Laramie.

"Woodpecker was *not* killed," said Pambrun, "though Tarno must have believed he was dead. Some Umatillas found the Nez Perce after he had lain in the sun for a day and the rain for a night—but still lived. They brought him to me. I have cared for him the best I could but he is still

174

far from well. The shooting occurred very soon after you left, which makes it look premeditated to me."

Pambrun took them to the room where Wookawkaw lay. In a corner sat an ancient squaw whom the trader had hired to care for the young Nez Perce. He was thin and hollow-eyed but he managed to smile. It was a ghost of his old wide grin.

"Poor Woodpecker!" exclaimed Nat in Nez Perce, dropping down beside him and gripping his hand. "But the captain is a *te-wats* who can soon make you well!"

"Don't promise too much," warned Captain Bonneville in English. He was already examining Wookawkaw's wound. "The bullet has passed clear through him," the captain reported. "There isn't much that surgery can do, except a better dressing of the wound. But it's nearly a month since he was shot. Surely if it were going to kill him, it would have done so by now."

"Chief-who-has-been-scalped, I took *good* care of your horses," Wookawkaw said earnestly. "I did nothing for which Square-jaw should have shot me."

"I am sure you did right," declared Captain Bonneville. "I cannot tell you," he went on bitterly, "how sorry I am that I left that man with you. I knew he was an unpleasant fellow but I fully believed he was honest. He fought loyally with us last summer."

"When de Crows would have taken *his* scalp, same as ours, eef we lost!" put in Laramie.

"I will fix you some medicine," the captain continued to Wookawkaw, "and teach this woman to take better care of you and give you stronger food. As soon as we reach the

175

Nez Perce villages, I will send some of your friends here for you. I am sure that by the time they arrive you will be able to return with them." Wookawkaw's smile answered that of the captain more strongly. Nat showed Woodpecker a hatchet and told him of watching the Hudson's Bay blacksmith forge and temper it especially for him, Nat. He was now passing the gift on to his friend.

Then the captain, Laramie and Nat went outside to face the fact that they were afoot and a long way from their friends the Nez Perces—a much longer way from Horse Prairie, where the captain was already due.

And such horses as they had lost! The captain's Hin-mot Hih-hih—White Thunder—a chief's gift. Laramie's spotted-rump Paloos that had brought him to within lance-length of many a buffalo, carried him out of many a danger. Nat's swift chestnut Kosooyeen—Going Alone. But greater than all other horses that walked was the pinto stallion. *His* pinto stallion that he had not even been able to claim! His Kiowa!

They found Pambrun busy receiving the goods brought to his post by the brigade. Captain Bonneville, remembering the refusal of all Hudson's Bay traders to do business with him, spoke stiffly but earnestly.

"I do not come to you now as a rival trader, Pambrun, but as a man eager to right a wrong. And as one wishing to do as you have done—help this young Indian to recover. I also come to you practically without funds. But if you can arrange to supply me with horses, I will send you their worth in beaver skins—also payment for your care of Wookawkaw. The skins are now with the Nez Perces, who

vill bring them when they come for their relative. In the
nterest of justice, I am sure you are eager for me to be
on the trail of this scoundrel, Tarno."

Pambrun left his duties and bought a horse apiece for
he three travelers from a nearby camp of Umatillas. He
ook the captain's note for the value of the horses but
refused to include anything for the care of Wookawkaw.

"The Company never charges for hospitality, or for help
of the sick or injured," the trader explained. He arranged
for the two Umatillas who had found Wookawkaw to
accompany the captain as far as needed, to help in the hunt
for Tarno's trail.

The best efforts of Laramie and the Indian trackers were
still unsure. A month of sun, wind and rain had straightened the bent grass. Near the site of the camp where the
shooting had occurred the later trail of a band of Indians
passed. Tarno's trail could not be followed with certainty
far enough to determine in which general direction he had
gone, although it was reasonable to expect him to take the
trail he knew—the trail on which the party had come west.
Captain Bonneville decided not to disregard the chance
that he had struck south with his loot, for in the distant
settlements of California a man with four exceptionally
fast horses might win larger bets in races, or sell for a
higher price, among the wealthy Spanish rancheros than at
a Rocky Mountain trappers' rendezvous.

So three days were spent in riding far and fast among
the Umatillas and Cayuses, through whose country Tarno
would have passed if he started for California. They

learned no word of a man with ten horses, including a white, a chestnut, a Paloos and a tall pinto.

"It's not proof that Tarno *didn't* go south," said the captain, "for by great luck he could have slipped through unnoticed. Or he might have been killed and the horses stolen. That, if I know Indians, would yield us this same gravelike silence from those we've questioned. But we can't spend more time here."

The party turned east.

"Tarno," said Laramie, "is bullheaded an' he look down his nose at all Injuns. But he's foxy ol' mount'in man an' he know he mus' kip outta sight wit' dose horses 'cause they're a prize few Injuns can resist. An' Tarno can't guard 'em both day an' night, nor w'ip whole band of Injuns he might meet. So he won't follow *any* trail more'n he have to. I think we should look for his trail away from de main trail. No?"

The captain agreed, so they still reined their impatience. They spread out and combed a wide strip of country on either side of the trail that led toward the Blue Mountains. They were conscious that Laramie might be wrong and that Tarno might have whipped his horses recklessly along the trail at four times the speed they were making, and thus was gaining more and more time to hide his plunder or to dispose of it.

So Nat and his companions gaunted their tough Indian horses. They took so little time for hunting game that the riders, too, were hungry more often than not. Ahead of them and a little higher each day were the Blue Mountains, so named because their timbered slopes were a dark

178

and distance-blued contrast to the gray-green and tawny tints of the flat miles of sage-and-grass land. When these mountains towered above them, the searchers still knew no more than they had known when they left Fort Walla Walla.

"I can't delay any longer!" exclaimed Captain Bonneville this night after their scanty supper. "I am already much too late to direct my trappers in the mountains around Horse Prairie in their spring beaver hunt. If I do not reach them before it is time to start for the summer trading rendezvous at Green River, they will consider me dead. They may disband and divide among themselves the fur they have taken as wages for their year's work. I've had enough losses lately so that without that fur and a profit from trade at the rendezvous, the business aspects of my expedition will be ruined. Tomorrow we take the trail as fast as we can ride."

And to Nat this meant that he might never know whether Tarno had taken Kiowa to the Rocky Mountains or to California!

That night, as on every night lately—but this time more strongly—Nat dreamed of horses . . . mostly of Kiowa. He dreamed he was a much smaller boy, back on Brent's farm, just learning to ride the strangely marked horse that Brent had brought home with him from Santa Fe. And then he was riding the pinto through the vast and lonely Teton Mountains, carrying the kit of surgical instruments to Captain Bonneville. And how he must hurry, to be in time to save Brent's life! Next he was on the brown horse

Pierre, beside Brent on Kiowa, thundering with the Black-feet into the war camp of the Crows.

That was where Nat had so nearly shot Far Eagle among the enemy. And now, these things that had really happened got mixed up with many more that were just as vivid—but real only in Nat's dream.

He was on Kiowa, pursuing Tarno toward the Blue Mountains, which also were running away. Tarno, on Kosooyeen, was leading Far Eagle, his prisoner. Half-dragging him, on foot and lame! Yet Kiowa wasn't over-taking them. Why? Because the pinto was hobbled and Nat thought he would lose sight of Tarno and Far Eagle if he got down to cut the thongs that tied the pinto's feet!

So Kiowa lurched along in clumsy, heartbreaking jumps until Tarno and Far Eagle slipped out of sight into the timbered canyons of the Blue Mountains, which they had overtaken at last. And Nat, almost crying with disappointment and vexation, was forced to hunt for their trail in order to follow them. Then, in the dream, the determined Kiowa took Nat to look for the trail in a pine-ringed meadow which Nat, in actuality, had been approaching at dusk the past evening. At which time the captain had joined the boy and given the order that they join Laramie and camp.

In the same way, before Nat reached the meadow in his dream he awoke. He was overheated with the provocation of his chase and shivering in anger at his stupidity in not cutting the hobbles on Kiowa. And burning with anger, too, at his good friend Captain Bonneville for preventing him, last evening, from reaching the meadow.

Perhaps the importance which the Indians ascribed to dreams, their belief that their totems or *wyakins* talked to them while they slept, doubled the vividness of this dream to Nat. He could not shake off the spell of it and he slipped out of his buffalo robe.

From the position of the Seven Persons, the Big Dipper, he knew it was nearly morning. By the time he could ride to that meadow, it would be light enough to see. The captain and his few companions kept no night guard here, for in this region no Indians were openly hostile to the whites. This little party had nothing to tempt any vagrant band to robbery. So Nat took his bow and quiver of arrows, quietly untied his horse from its picket line and rode away.

When he found the meadow it was light enough for him to know that horses had been picketed there. He counted the circles where the grass, though it had straightened, was shorter than the uncropped grass nearby. There were ten. That was the number of the horses taken by Tarno. The picket pins had been pulled up. Why, except to make the spot less conspicuous? Nat found one of the pins in the edge of the timber. Its sharpened point was browned by what looked to have been the sun and rain of about a month. That was the length of time that Tarno was ahead of them.

Still, this was not positive evidence. Searching farther, Nat found a little spot of ashes in the timber, marking the place of a one-night camp. He was certain he would have known the blunt print of Tarno's moccasins but the springy pine needles held no clear track.

The soft ground of the meadow still held hoofprints and these Nat studied carefully. He found large ones, long with open heels. Like Kiowa's. If Nat had seen them in a trail, he could have been sure. He had followed Kiowa's tracks too many miles not to know exactly how much the hind feet of the long-striding stallion overstepped his front ones. But from a hoofprint here and there . . .

Then Nat saw a spot where the hoofs of one of the horses had cut entirely through the meadow sod into the mud beneath. Among these tracks was one which showed on one side a vertical ridge such as would have been made by a crease in the hoof. He could remember with certainty that it was the near front foot of Kosooyeen—the foot on the side from which one mounted—that had been split . . . split on the outside by the rocky trail along Snake River. Going Alone's lameness had disappeared more than a month ago but the crease would not grow entirely out of his hoof for a year. Now Nat knew, as though he had seen him, that the horse picketed here was his chestnut, Kosooyeen.

Turning back, Nat soon met the captain and Laramie hunting for him. He took a sharp rebuke for leaving camp in the way he had done. But then he led them to the meadow. There they checked all Nat's findings.

Laramie said, "As a sign reader, you're gettin' to be a reg'lar Injun, Big Medicine. At last we know for sure dat Tarno is ahead of us." The captain nodded and admitted he was glad for the persistence of Nat.

They sent the two Umatillas home. After but a few hours' travel beyond the spot where the pursuers took up the trail they had so long been seeking, Tarno had found it necessary to join the trail that led through the pass in the Blue Mountains. But he did so by bringing his horses, tied in a line head to tail, down the rocky bed of a creek. Tarno entered the trail where it forded the stream. If Nat and his companions had not found his trail before it reached this point, they could not have recognized it afterwards, for the hoofs of horses ridden by more recent travelers had blotted all earlier tracks.

Apparently Tarno had passed through the Blue Mountains without encountering anyone. And beyond their peaks and canyons he must have left the trail again in some manner like that by which he entered it, for in the Wallowa Valley, as it was soon learned from the Nez Perces, Tarno and his stolen horses had not been seen.

←≪ ←≪ ←≪ CHAPTER **13**

Lost Beaver

The Nex Perces in each of the valleys through which the captain, Laramie and Nat now passed were shocked to learn that their friend, the Chief-who-has-been-scalped, had suffered so by Square-jaw's treachery. And they were much aroused over his nearly successful attempt to kill Wookawkaw. Though Tarno had successfully detoured the Wallowa and Imnaha valleys, there could be little doubt that he had attempted to cross the Snake River Mountains by the trail over which Wookawkaw had led the captain and his party during the early winter. There was no other. But it would be an amazing thing if he got through.

To the captain's good fortune, a band of Nez Perce braves offered to go with him. These were young men who were already planning to start soon for the buffalo country—much earlier than usual this year, in order to attend the rendezvous. Their object was not trade but to take part in the horse racing, which was always a great feature of this gathering of Indians of many tribes. They were waiting only for the snow to melt in the high passes of the mountains. They were willing to attempt an earlier crossing for the sake of getting started sooner on the trail of Tarno.

The Nez Perces were not a vengeful people. But they were not a sort to let wrongs go unpunished. It was the deepest humiliation to Captain Bonneville that *this* wrong —the first injustice that these Indians had ever received at the hands of a white man—should have been the work of a member of his own party in whom he had placed confidence.

The warriors came from the different villages to the number of thirty-six, led by a young chief named Ten Owl. It would be only fair to them to say that a large part of their motive was to help their friend the captain recover, if possible, his goods and stolen horses, particularly the white one given him by Speaking Thunder, a Nez Perce chief. In addition, five older men led by Red Wolf, who chanced at present to be in the village of Tu-eka-kas, agreed to start soon for Fort Walla Walla, to bring Wookawkaw home to his own people. To these captain Bonneville gave a liberal number of beaver skins from his store left with Tu-eka-kas, to pay them for their trip. He also entrusted to them the skins to pay his debt to Pambrun.

Ten Owl was a relative of Wookawkaw but as different as could be from that happy-go-lucky fellow. His handsome features were lean as a hawk's, and just as stern. He spoke seldom, was obeyed immediately. It was weeks be-

fore Nat saw him smile. The white boy admired him and
tried to get to know him, but without much success.

Fresh horses were willingly traded to Captain Bonneville for his three trail-gaunted ones, and he was offered
the loan of as many more as he needed to pack his beaver
skins. The three horses which he had left here were caught
for him. One of these was Whitefoot and Nat was glad
to see the bay again.

He was also more than glad to see Hin-mot Too-yah-
lah-kekt, his friend Rainbow—and Hin-mot's mother,
Swan Woman. Their welcome to Strongbow lifted Nat, for
the time at least, from his loneliness for Brent and his
anxiety for Kosooyeen and Kiowa. He had much to tell
these friends of his journey to the Columbia and his voyage
down that great river to Fort Vancouver. The chief wonder
to them was that of the ship.

"A-a-ah!" they exclaimed. "What keeps the big sail-
canoe, when it goes beyond the sunset, from falling off the
edge of the world?"

Nat had long been turning over in his mind the idea of
sending a gift to Cecille. He realized that the trip of Red
Wolf and his men to get Wookawkaw offered him his one
chance. So, at the price of considerable teasing from Swan
Woman, he had her secure for him, somewhere in the
village, one of the little brimless hats woven of colored
grasses which the Nez Perce girls and women wore, and a
pair of moccasins, beaded the most beautifully of any that
he had ever seen.

Nat had another embarrassing moment when he told

Captain Bonneville of his purchase and asked the captain to address the package. Brent had taught Nat how to write but even Brent had original notions of spelling and the boy knew that his own were still more unreliable. Smiling indulgently—while Laramie's look was rather sour—the captain took ink and a goose-quill pen from the box in which he kept his records and wrote with bold flourishes:

Mademoiselle Cecille St. Anns
French Prairie Settlement
via Fort Vancouver, Oregon
By courtesy of Hudson's Bay Co. Express

It looked admirably imposing and Nat carried it to Red Wolf with instructions that he place it in the hands only of Trader Pambrun.

Early the next morning, Nat said good-by to his Nez Perce friends, this time wondering with a good deal of sadness if he would ever see them again.

"Come back, Strongbow," said Tu-eka-kas.

"You will come back," said Swans-lighting-on-the-water and Thunder-rolling-to-higher-mountaintops.

Captain Bonneville and his party, so greatly reinforced by the Nez Perces and all their extra horses, made a long cavalcade that filed across the Valley of Winding Waters and the beautiful Imnaha. They wound from ridge to higher ridge of the Snake River Mountains. Though the snow was melting fast, they found it still very deep, and growing deeper as they went. They could see that, many days ahead of them, horses had been over this trail. Much snow had fallen since but the trough wallowed out by the

187

previous travelers showed in the thicker parts of the timber where the wind had not drifted the snow.

Traveling was now at its worst, for the deep snow was soggy and wet. Along most of the way, a crew of men had to tramp back and forth over each section of the trail before the first of the horses could be led over it. Still it was an exhausting flounder, for their small hoofs let them sink to their bellies in the heavy snow. However, because there were many men and horses, the trail breakers could be changed often. The leaders fell out and let the followers take their places. In the rear of the long file, the trail was well packed and there was a chance to become rested, somewhat, before they worked up to the head of the column again.

"But what a job it would have been for just three of us, and only a few horses!" puffed the captain.

"*Morbleu!* We play out. Come night we freeze," said Laramie. " 'Fore long, we find Tarno an' his hosses in snow up to their gills an' hard as logs."

Still they plowed on and Laramie's dire prophecy did not come true—quite. They did find three horses, dead in the trail. They had been good horses, but the poorest of the stolen herd. While Laramie and the captain marveled that Tarno had not even abandoned the trade goods he was assumed to still be carrying, Ten Owl explained that a month earlier, when Tarno had passed, the weather had been much colder. That was a great advantage to him because then the snow was dry and feathery and a horse could breast his way through it, where now it packed around him and resisted his every move. Still it seemed unbe-

lievable that Tarno could make it over the summit . . .
unbelievable to everyone but Nat. Only he had such faith
in Kiowa.

Kiowa, he told himself, would break trail when the rest
could barely follow! But beyond doubt, Tarno was made
of iron, too.

And Tarno and his horses did make it; over the mountains and down their farther side. He crossed the Snake
River by the help of the canoe cached by Wookawkaw when
the party had been journeying west. On the lava plains
farther upriver, he lost another horse. But he met a band
of Shoshonies well loaded with fur. Captain Bonneville
and those with him also found these Indians, camped by
the river and living on northward-bound geese. The
Shoshonies had the trade goods that had belonged to the
captain. They said that, in exchange, Tarno now had dried
buffalo meat, three fresh horses and five packs of beaver—
about three hundred skins. He also had six companions—
young, venturesome warriors who wished to visit another
band of their tribe whom they expected to meet at the
rendezvous.

And Tarno was twenty days ahead!

The Shoshonies were very sorry to learn of Captain
Bonneville's losses. More exactly, they were uneasy with
the thought that he might reclaim as much as possible of
his goods. How could they have known, they repeated
many times, that the square-jawed trader was a thief?
Being assured that nothing would be seized from them,
they gave wild geese and the last of their pemmican to the
captain and his friends. The food was welcome, for all

were hungry, but it was accepted rather stiffly by the Nez Perces. The Shoshoni and the Nez Perce tribes were not friends. However, since they had a deadly common enemy in the Blackfeet, they did not fight each other very often. Captain Bonneville hurried on with the Nez Perces, glad to put space between the two groups before old grievances were remembered by either side.

His band entered the western limits of the buffalo range. Now they were in country where they were likely to encounter enemies. Scouts rode in advance, on the flanks and to the rear of the party. Guards were posted at night. But no Indians were seen—and no buffalo, until they were nearly to Horse Prairie. Then they came upon the greatest herd Nat had seen since he left the plains of the Platte River, the summer before. The shaggy beasts, scattered only enough to graze, darkened the prairie for miles. They were restless, for the sky was overcast, threatening a storm.

The buffalo were all bulls, for in the spring and early summer, bulls and cows ranged in separate herds. The air vibrated with the near-and-far rumble of their bellowing, a sound that blended with the growl of thunder coming from the edges of the sky.

Quick preparations for a chase were made by the Indians. Nat did not expect to take part, knowing that only a few buffalo were needed for immediate eating. This was the season when the buffalo were shedding—not the time to take hides for robes. Also, there was no chance now, or need, to dry meat. And Indians, unlike so many white men, did not waste game for sport.

Ten Owl gave a nod to each of the few warriors he had

selected to kill buffalo. The young chief had shown so little interest in Nat that the white boy was startled now to hear his name.

"Strongbow." It was said with the faintest hint of sarcasm. Nat knew that the unsmiling Ten Owl thought that he had been overrated. He was being put to a test.

He strung his horn bow and selected his broadest tipped arrows. He rode forward quietly with four Nez Perces. The buffalo, already on the alert because of the approaching storm, broke into a run while the hunters were still far from them. The horses skimmed forward. Nat knew it would be a long run, for no matter how lumbering was the appearance of a buffalo's gallop, the gait covered ground at an astonishing rate.

Nat had been riding Whitefoot all morning. He was not so fresh or so fast as the special buffalo horses of the Nez Perces. They left him in their dust, which was soon mixed with the dust raised by the thundering buffalo as more and more of the great herd broke into a run.

"*Ai-i-i-i! Ai-i-i-i!*"

Ahead of him, Nat heard the yells of the other hunters as they overtook the buffalo, selected their victims and launched their arrows. He was only beginning to see through the brown dust the brown humps of the buffalo. With bearded heads low, they ran, ponderous, shaggy shoulders bounding, tails erect above short-haired hindquarters that dwindled until they seemed made for some other sort of an animal. Now, out of these countless bobbing blurs, he must select a *young* bull; a fat one! Nat

191

rode neck-or-nothing for a long way farther before he made his choice.

It was a task just to keep in sight of the one he had selected—a greater task to close Whitefoot in, almost to arm's length, on the bull's right flank. Nat didn't know whether the little bay had ever hunted buffalo. The horse showed no fear, though. Nat tensed to the question—did Whitefoot show fear enough? Was he watching the bull alertly, as a good buffalo horse must, ready to leap away if the buffalo threw himself to one side? Those curving black horns could rip a horse's flank like it was rabbit skin. That thick neck could toss Whitefoot over on top of Nat and under the hoofs of the older, heavier bulls they had already passed.

Nat set an arrow. Legs clamped to Whitefoot's barrel, he put all his strength into one flash of movement that drew the arrow to its head and let it go.

"*Ai-i-i-i-i!*" He was not conscious of his yell until his ears told him.

Nat's right hand whipped another arrow from the top of his quiver, above his right shoulder. That, too, he launched. Even now, the power of the horn bow surprised him. Only the feathers of the two arrows showed, low in the bull's forward flank.

The bull stumbled, went on. His tongue lolled and his nostrils were blowing blood. Nat was trying to check Whitefoot when the buffalo swerved in a sudden, furious charge.

The tired Whitefoot was *not* watching the bull as a trained buffalo horse would have been, but he *was* alert to

192

the swing of Nat's weight and the fierce thump of his heels. He jumped clear of the black horns—barely. He kept his feet, leaping sideways on the rough ground. And the buffalo went down, to stay.

The rest of the herd, in a growing wave, was rolling on across the prairie. A sudden gust of wind helped carry away the dust. In the wind came a pelting of big raindrops. A long ways behind him, Nat could see his companion hunters, each well along with his task of butchering. Nat ran his knife in a long slit down the back of the beast he had killed—the way to start on a buffalo when saving the hide was no object. He saw the white fat over the loin and knew he need make no excuses. Ten Owl rode up, saw the fat and saw Nat draw out his two arrows by their heads from the farther flank of the buffalo.

He said, *"Taats!"* which meant "good." *That* was the first time Nat saw him smile.

It sent a ripple of elation through the boy, but not so keenly as had the approval of Swift Bear when he and Far Eagle had each killed their first buffalo with a bow. Nat was already wise enough to know that for any sort of experience there can be only one *first*. But this thrill renewed his determination to hunt again with Far Eagle— with Far Eagle as a companion and with the powerful, well-trained Kiowa between his knees.

But just now thrills of any sort were quenched in a slash of rain. Whitefoot swung his rump to it and lowered his head, while Nat worked doggedly on at his butchering; soaked, hammered, cold, seeing blue-white sometimes from the lightning and jarred by the thunder that seemed just over his head.

A Nez Perce sent by Ten Owl helped him finish his job. They packed all the best of the meat on the two horses the Indian had brought. Typically, by this time the storm had passed and shafts of sunlight came through the torn clouds.

That night there was prodigious feasting on roast hump-ribs, sirloins and buffalo tongues. But stuffed though the Indians were, Captain Bonneville and Ten Owl made sure that they kept an alert guard. Blackfeet, Gros Ventres, Bannecks, Pen d'Oreilles, Utes, Shoshonies—some friendly and some decidedly not—might, any or all of them, be in the region of this great buffalo herd.

They were still near the Snake River and this night's camp was not far from the spot where Captain Bonneville had made his caches. Nat recalled how the robbing of one of these had been an early event in a train of losses that would have completely discouraged any man of a less staunch and determined character than his admired friend.

The next day they reached the spot designated by the captain for a meeting with his men. Much camping had been done here by white men—undoubtedly his men waiting for his return. Some windowless, earth-roofed log huts had even been built. The place had been occupied the very night just passed but it was deserted now. Captain Bonneville took up the trail of about twenty horses.

The captain and his Indian friends set their horses at a fast trot, which was as swift a pace as could be held for a long distance. After covering about five miles, they could see the party of trappers they were following, specks on the

194

horizon. In another five miles they had gained enough to be noticed by the band in the lead. The trappers, recognizing that they were being pursued by a band much larger than their own and undoubtedly Indians, now made all possible speed toward a distant creek and the shelter of its fringe of timber.

With the rest, Nat spurred his horse, and another two miles of sagebrush plain swept underneath him. The fast Nez Perce horses had now brought their riders to within half a mile of the fugitives, whose few pack horses were heavily loaded. The smaller band saw that they could not win their race to the creek so they stopped abruptly and prepared to defend themselves on the open plain.

Swiftly they unpacked their horses and tied the animals' heads close together, in groups of five or six. The men formed a ring around the horses and each one piled his packs into a low barricade, then lay down behind this. . . . The band silently waited for the expected charge to come within range.

But the pursuers also stopped. The captain, Laramie and Nat rode forward, each holding his right hand above his head in the white man's sign of peace. Soon they were recognized and shouts of surprised welcome went up from the trappers. They advanced to meet the captain as he approached.

"Skin me fer a drowned beaver, Cap'n," said their leader, "but we thought ye'd gone under!" It was Fenton, the lieutenant or "partisan." He was a short man, wearing a broad white hat. While the twelve men with him had beards in varying degrees of shagginess, Fenton was smooth-shaven, except for a long, drooping mustache that gave him a sad expression. But without it, Nat guessed, he wouldn't look happy, either.

"Where's Brent an' Tarno?" Fenton asked.

"Logan fell," answered the captain, "not to lead or arrows but to feminine charms. He has taken a wife and a farm in the Oregon settlements. But I'll ask *you* for news of Tarno. Have you seen or heard of him?"

"Nary hoof nor sound. Pull out on ye?"

Tersely the captain told the part that had been played by Tarno. There were words of surprise and contempt from the trappers, and a few nods and "I told you so's" between man and man. By hindsight, it was easy for them to read Tarno's untrustworthy character, although actually while among them he had been merely gruff and hard.

Captain Bonneville signaled the Nez Perces to join them, speaking of these Indians to the men around him in the highest terms. Finally, the trappers saddled and packed their horses.

"Where do we join the rest of our men?" the captain asked as they rode forward.

"Well-er, probably down at the rendezvous." Fenton seemed in no hurry to explain why he had only one-fourth of his original fifty men with him. Or why these had less than one pack horse apiece loaded with beaver skins. Captain Bonneville asked for a full account of the winter's operations. Nat, riding in his usual place beside the captain, heard all of it.

The fall trapping had been fairly successful, Fenton said, although some of the bands of trappers had found

196

themselves preceded by rival trappers of the American Fur Company. Other bands had been driven from the grounds they had started to trap by Indians, presumably Blackfeet. A man named Kershaw had been captured and killed, and some traps and horses lost. But when they went into winter quarters, a thousand prime beaver plew had been stored in their camp.

They had wintered well. Buffalo had remained in the region in sufficient numbers to keep them from going hungry and the snow had not become so deep as to make it difficult for their horses to paw through it to graze. It was with the approach of spring that difficulties had set in.

Indians, again presumed to be Blackfeet, had run off more than half their horses. In answer to the captain's sharp questioning, Fenton admitted that the horses had not been guarded nor the loss even discovered for several days. By that time it was decided that the chance of recovering the horses was too small to be worth the risk of being ambushed, if they attempted to follow the Indians. From here on the story was a sorry one.

"Hired trappers," Fenton reminded the captain, "are gener'ly the culls o' the mountain men, without the nerve or the savvy to go it on their own. Men among 'em like Brent Logan or Laramie, here, are scarce as feathered frogs. When Blackfeet were believed to be near us, more'n half the men I had with me got chicken-livered. They remembered findin' Kershaw, stuck full o' pitch-pine splinters an' burned. We were all mighty short o' hosses, besides."

Fenton went on to tell that in his determination to make some showing for the captain and to perhaps shame some of the timid trappers to action, he had led a party consisting mostly of the men now with him, clear to the Malade River. They had outguessed both Indians and rival trappers and brought back the fur now in their possession —more than four hundred plew. But on his return, Fenton learned news that made him wish he had never set out.

Only a few other bands of trappers had left the safety of numbers at the winter camp. These had not gone far enough to take much fur. The idle group had to eat, however, and so were compelled to stage an occasional buffalo hunt. One party of hunters, some ten days previous, had been fired on by Indians when they were still within hearing of the camp.

The Indians had been crafty enough to first cut off the hunters' retreat to camp, and had also chosen hilly ground where they could, for the most part, remain hidden. But their attack was a blustery one, not much like the swift, deadly work of Blackfeet. The men in the camp heard the sound of the battle and all hurried to the aid of their comrades. The Indians had been driven off. These trappers who wouldn't trap had returned to camp, elated.

They had returned to find that all the packs of fur taken in the fall hunt had been carried off!

Fenton paused. Everyone expected a stormy outburst from the captain. "Go on," was all he said.

"Not many o' those men," Fenton resumed, "had any stomach for meetin' you, Cap'n, after that. Nor even the face to draw their wages. That is—if you *did* return. Which none of 'em expected, you bein' two months overdue. So our brave *compañeros* swapped some of your powder an' galena to some friendly Bannecks fer enough hosses to git all of 'em off their ankles, an' started fer the rondyvoo at Green River. Most of 'em figger to make their way back to St. Louie with Sublette an' Campbell's fall brigade. Good riddance, I'd say, if it weren't such a ruinous expensive one! It sure gripes my gizzard to hev to tell you all this, on top the bad luck you've already had."

Laramie expressed his opinion of the spineless trappers in an outburst of stormy English and French, either of which language possessed more words of contempt than any of the Indian tongues he knew. But Captain Bonneville continued silent and Nat, with all his admiration for his friend, was surprised that he could do so. The Nez Perces, when they heard the news, clucked their tongues and shook their heads. Nat was ashamed to think of how their high opinion of white men must have fallen recently.

When Captain Bonneville did speak, his voice was neither angry nor complaining. "It will not bring back the fur to remind you once again, Fenton," he said, "that *nothing* takes the place of constant preparedness. A guard on your horse herd, no matter how safe you thought you were, might have prevented the whole train of sorry events. But I take the larger share of the blame. These losses are the price of my explorations. The practical thing would have been to stay here and direct my trapping. Well, before we leave this region, let's try to learn whether there's a chance to reclaim any of our loss."

They were now near the creek which the trappers had been attempting to reach when they were overtaken. They stopped for a noon camp.

Among the men with Fenton were three who had not gone with him to the Malade River but had tried to lead other trapping parties—tried unsuccessfully, because of the mutinous fear that possessed their followers. With the rest, they had been fooled into leaving camp to repulse the sham attack on the buffalo hunters. But they were of too sturdy a nature to run away after the fur was lost. It was they who had reported the disaster to Fenton and they faced Captain Bonneville's questions now.

"Did you learn to what tribe the Indians belonged who made this fake attack?"

A lanky fellow called Kaintuck, who seemed the most competent and reliable mountain man, answered.

"We winged one Injun an' he fell offen his hoss. He hopped on agin, but where he stood the ground was soft fr'm the meltin' o' the snow. I looked good at his tracks an' he wore moccasins cut in the Shoshoni style."

"But the Shoshonies are friendly!"

"I kain't hep that, Cap'n. You ast me what I seen."

"Did you, even from a distance, see the ones who raided the camp?"

"Nope. But I found the tracks o' their hosses where they crossed the crick, after takin' off with the beaver plew. I covered some o' the tracks with chunks o' pine bark to show Fenton when he came. But he said hoss tracks hadn't any sale value. The fur was gone, we didn't hev enough men to whup the Blackfeet, an' that was that."

Fenton nodded, standing by his line of reasoning.

"But I want Laramie and Nat and my Nez Perce friends to see them," said the captain. "We will return."

200

Nat could hear some of the men grumbling that twenty miles was a long ways for sixteen men, "besides thirty-six Injuns who don't count," to ride back to look at some horse tracks. There were thousands of horses in the region, all much the same size, all unshod. But they reached the site of the winter camp by sunset. It was still light under the trees by the creek and Nat, Laramie, Ten Owl and a few other of the Nez Perces went with the captain, Fenton and Kaintuck. The tracks were in a mud bar and the covers of pine bark had protected them from the recent rain, so that they were as clear as when made.

"Horses come long ways," said Ten Owl at once.

Nat knew that the hoofs of most horses grew long during the winter, when they were not traveling very much—except that they were generally worn off straight across the front of the fore feet only, from pawing for grass under the snow. But he saw quickly that both fore and hind hoofs of the horses that had made these tracks were worn down all around, almost even with the soles of their feet. Like the hoofs of their own horses and those of the Nez Perces, that had recently crossed the Snake River lava plains.

At this point Laramie broke out with a *"Sacre!"* over a track that seemed to mean much—if only to him. Then Nat gulped with equal excitement over a track that was longer than the rest, with open heels. The next moment he was pointing conclusively to the print of a near forefoot that had the mark of a crease in the outside of the hoof.

Captain Bonneville, Laramie and Nat spoke the same word simultaneously.

"Tarno!"

Square-jaw—as it was explained to Ten Owl—Square-jaw, with some one to help him, must have taken the fur, for Kiowa, Kosooyeen and Laramie's Paloos were among the horses that had packed away the sixteen bales of skins.

Laramie pointed out the distinguishing features of the tracks to Ten Owl, who called all his warriors to make mental notes for future use.

"So it wasn't for horse racing—at least not alone for racing," commented Captain Bonneville, "that Tarno took such risks to secure the fastest horses he could find! He wanted them for whatever deviltry like this might come his way. Now, with his loot more than doubled, where has he gone?"

Captive

"Tarno, I think, won't take fur to de rendezvous," Laramie said in partial answer to Captain Bonneville's question. "Ev'rybody would know dat a hired trapper couldn't bring in thirteen hunner beaver plew in one year —honestly. An' how he know he don't find us dere, ready to shoot him for stealin' our horses?"

"What else might he do with the fur, if he doesn't sell it at the rendezvous?" the captain questioned. They had started toward the fire the trappers had lighted.

"Many things. Could sell it at Henry's Fort on de upper Missouri. Could take it 'way south to Bent's Fort on de Arkansas. More likely he take it to St. Louie himself."

"Across the plains?"

"Mebbe. He got good horses. Or mebbe he go to Big-horn River in de Crow country. Make boat of willow frame covered wit' buffalo hides. Float down Bighorn to Yellowstone, down Yellowstone to Missouri, thousand mile down Missouri to St. Louie."

"Could either such trip be made by one man?"

"*Oui*—yes. Mighty risky, but Tarno been takin' big chances all along."

"Tarno isn't a canoeman," objected the captain.

"He isn't a horseman, neither," said Nat, sharply.

"Dat's right, both times," agreed Laramie. "But he can get long ways on de good horses he's got 'fore he kill 'em off. An' you, *Capitaine*, are thinkin' 'bout w'en we're at Fort Walla Walla—Tarno just say he *didn't want* five hunner mile canoe ride. But he led his horses across Snake River in dat little Injun dugout. Lotsa men have floated down de Missouri in bullboats w'en, at de start, they knew as much about canoes as this beaver knows about balloons." He added soberly, "Lotsa men have started—an' been shot by Arickaras, too."

Fenton took his first part in the discussion. "You're lookin' beyant the skyline when your answer is under your feet," he said. "Tarno is in cahoots with that band of American Fur Comp'ny men that have been plaguing us all season. They riled up the Blackfeet to run you out o' the Roubidoux's River valley last fall, Cap'n. That was stric'ly Blackfoot kentry. But even here in the Portneuf an' Banneck Mount'ins, where we've as much right as anyone, the presence o' that band o' whites an' their way o' smashin' beaver lodges when they've caught as many beaver as they're smart enough to trap has kep' the Blackfeet buzzin' like hornets all year.

"Must be," he continued, "that Comp'ny outfit stayed together in a party too big fer the Injuns to whip, is why they taken it out on us. Anyway, I betcha it was Tarno sent 'em word o' the location of your cache that was robbed. Betcha he's already turned the beaver he stole over to them."

Laramie put in a word here. " 'Member de night de Crows run off our horses? Tarno was gone hour or so—an' Brent tol' me he *didn't* help get de horses back. Mebbe he was talkin' to dem Crows. Dey might have been in pay of American Fur Comp'ny, too."

The discussion continued after they reached the camp. It was all guess, except that Tarno had the help of someone in staging the attack which gave him the chance to steal the fur. It was remembered that Tarno hired, or otherwise persuaded, six Shoshonies to accompany him, from the band near the Snake River with whom he had also traded the captain's goods for five packs of beaver skins.

At daylight, everyone in the camp took up the trail.

"Here's once we'll have no trouble to follow the signs," said Nat to Laramie, and he pointed with satisfaction to Ten Owl and some of his Nez Perce trackers taking the lead. Laramie moved his head doubtfully.

"Wait till we get beyond de soft earth of dis creek valley," he said. "On sod of de hard prairie, dat storm which wet your buffalo hunt, she'll dim dis trail." This prophecy proved true. Even to travel at a walk kept the trackers working diligently. But they continued for five or six patient miles. The general direction was westward, down the Snake River, instead of the expected northeast toward the Bighorn, or southeast toward the rendezvous.

Then a more recent trail of many horses covered the sign of Tarno where it went through a pass in some hills.

205

Beyond the pass, on a vast open prairie, it could not be distinguished again.

The newer trail Ten Owl pronounced to be that of a Blackfoot war party. More trails were encountered, made that same morning. Trails of scouts, Ten Owl said. He and his warriors showed that a sense of danger was growing on them, for they put on their eagle-plume headdresses for the protection they believed this gave them. They also took from their medicine bundles their bone war whistles and their *kopluts* or short war clubs. Scouts were thrown out on either flank and in the rear.

Tarno's trail being lost, they could only ride on up the miles-wide floor of the valley. A watchful hour passed. Ten Owl put up his hand to halt the party and sent two small bands of his warriors riding swiftly to encircle, from either side, a rocky butte rising on the left.

"What do you see?" asked Captain Bonneville.

"See nothing—now," Nat heard the answer. "But did see shadow, up in those rocks. Shadow of the top of a warrior's head. Shoshoni, by the way he wore his feather."

Nat was used to men of keen eyesight and observation, but for anyone to make such an identification from a shadow two hundred yards away seemed incredible. Then the two detachments of Nez Perces came back in one group from beyond the butte. In their midst and disarmed were five Shoshoni warriors. One had a half-healed wound on the side of his head. Not knowing what to expect, their faces were expressionless. But their eyes brightened when the captain questioned them, through Laramie.

They said they were from a band that lived many

"sleeps" westward, along Snake River. A square-jawed white man from the west had traded with their band for fur and had given six of them trinkets to accompany him. They had staged the "noise battle" on the trappers. But the white man, with one of their number, had disappeared. They, too, were trying to find Square-jaw. They wanted the extra pay he had promised them and they wanted their fellow tribesman. Then they would go toward the rendez-vous—would go quickly from this region where they had seen sign of so many Blackfeet lately.

When the Shoshonies had seen the captain's party in the distance, they had supposed them to be more Blackfeet and had hidden on the butte to watch them pass. Their faces grew anxious when they learned it was from Captain Bon-neville that Tarno, with their help, had stolen a great many beaver skins. But he assured them that now he only wanted their aid in finding this Square-jaw. He ordered their bows, their smooth-bore fusees and their knives re-turned to them.

More miles passed under the hoofs of the party. In front of the captain and the trappers, Laramie and the Indians spread in a line, still searching the storm-beaten sod for the trail of Tarno. More tracks of Blackfoot scouts were seen but no glimpse of the riders who had made them.

Then an object on the ground held the Nez Perces' attention from a distance until they reached it. A ring of them formed around it. The captain and Nat spurred forward.

Nearing the group, they heard a dreary sound that be-gan just above a whisper and rose in volume. It came from

the throats of the five Shoshonies. The object on the
ground had once been the sixth member of their group.
He had not been scalped, as he would have been had he
met death by the hand of an Indian. He lay as he had
fallen from his horse when a bullet in the back had killed
him.

The body was beside the trail of seven horses and they
had passed since the storm of two days ago. Nat, remembering what had happened to Wookawkaw, was not surprised to find proof that this was the trail of Tarno. The
proof was the long-striding tracks of Kiowa. The Nez
Perces, who had seen the tracks of the pinto stallion in the
mud near the trappers' camp, agreed with Nat.

With a trail that, at last, was easy to see, the party took
it up at a gallop . . . except the five Shoshonies. They
remained behind to dig with their knives and fingers a
grave in the hard plain. They would put stones above the
body of their comrade to discourage coyotes, then ride their
horses many times over the spot to hide it from scalp-
crazy enemies.

Now the captain and his men had the trail they sought
and could see it distinctly. . . . They had followed it less
than an hour when a blur on the plain ahead of them grew,
as they neared it, into many moving men and horses—
riders swinging in a circle. Plainly a battle was in progress
between a large number of Indians and a besieged band of
trappers.

Captain Bonneville swung his party to the assistance of
the white men.

The attacking Blackfoot Indians, seeing a charge sweep-

CAPTIVE

ing down on them, broke their circle. They were not outnumbered. There were at least a hundred of them. Captain Bonneville's men and the Nez Perces numbered fifty-two. There were twenty-five trappers forted up behind their fur packs. This made a total of less than eighty. But though the Blackfeet were quick to see their own numerical superiority, they had no mind to be caught between two forces. Also, numbers were not the only consideration. They had respect for the accurate rifles of the fifteen more white men whom they could count in the reinforcing party. The situation called for a pause to consider the changed conditions.

They stood off, just out of rifle range. While their chiefs took council, the ranks kept up a ferocious yelling, emphasized by the occasional *whoom* of a fusee. Indians were great users of "psychological warfare," long before anyone invented that name for bluff.

Captain Bonneville, also, was glad of a chance to size up the fight into which he had plunged.

"Who are you?" he asked a large man in a worn blue capote who stepped forward as partisan of the besieged trappers. The hood of the capote hung down the man's back. His shaggy, sunburned hair reached his shoulders and his beard swept his breast.

"I'm Andy Birlock. We're American Fur Comp'ny men, but what's that matter? The red devils outnumber us, so we're right glad to see ye, Cap'n Bonneville."

The man said this with a hearty voice and a steady eye that surprised Nat. He remembered all that Birlock's band had done to provoke the Blackfeet, first against Captain

209

Bonneville, then his trappers. The Blackfeet had at last gathered sufficient force to wipe out the entire band of American Fur Company men, even though they were now beyond the limits of acknowledged Blackfoot land.

Then something else gave Nat a quicker intake of breath. It was recognition of the blue capote Birlock was wearing. The blanket-coth coat was dirty now, but by its trimming of gold braid Nat knew it was one that Captain Bonneville had ordered specially made in St. Louis. He very well remembered packing it into one of the caches—the one that had been robbed. Nat realized that the captain recognized the capote and that Birlock knew that he did. It identified Birlock as the thief, and there was small excuse that cache robbing was a not infrequent part of the cutthroat rivalry of mountain trade. Still the hard eyes of the burly partisan did not waver.

Captain Bonneville—and Nat and Laramie with him—scrutinized the rest of the American Fur Company men. All were unfamiliar. Of the twenty-five, three were already seriously wounded. The captain turned back to Birlock and the eyes of Nat and Laramie went on to the group of horses, four of which were down. It was an inadequate herd for the men and their packs of skins and Nat thought they must already have lost a number to the Blackfeet.

"Have you seen a man named Tarno?" Captain Bonneville asked Birlock.

"No," was the solid answer.

"Dat's a lie." For Laramie, the words were said very calmly.

CAPTIVE

Birlock whirled on him. "Fightin' words, Frenchy. Git offen that hoss."

"Stop it!" commanded the captain.

"But Laramie's right!" Nat broke in. "There's my chestnut, Kosooyeen, among the trappers' horses. Tarno had him and how else could he be here, if Tarno didn't bring him?" The chestnut took two steps and in doing so painfully threw up his head. In distress, Nat exclaimed, "Oh, he's lame again! Maybe that's why Tarno left him here."

Faced with this evidence, Birlock grudgingly admitted that Tarno had lately been in his party.

"He brought you about thirteen hundred beaver skins. *My* beaver skins," stated Captain Bonneville.

"He didn't bring a plew!" declared Birlock, hotly.

"Check that," said the captain to Laramie.

Swiftly Laramie and Nat examined the packs of skins in possession of this party. Captain Bonneville had given Fenton a small punch and with it the nose of each dried beaver skin was pierced with four little holes, before the skins were pressed into packs.

"None o' your plew here," reported Laramie.

"Told you he didn't bring any," said Birlock. "Just came and demanded pay."

"For sending word to you of my plans, so you could head me off. For telling you the location of my cache." This time the captain's aim was accurate.

"All right—yes!" Birlock's voice was gritty, his tone defiant. "I wouldn't pay him . . . not till we reached rondyvoo. He took another hoss in place o' that lame one

211

an' stole a pack o' beaver plew an' sneaked off, night before last. But Roarin' Moses, let's git on with fightin' Blackfeet! Ef we give 'em a volley of slugs right now, while they're still chewin' the fat, an' your Naypercys charge into 'em—good chance they'll scatter 'em."

"I do not intend that any of my men shall fight the Blackfeet," said Captain Bonneville.

"Wha-at?" At last Birlock was staggered—momentarily.

"For three reasons," continued the captain. "First, I fought *with* the Blackfeet last summer. I have friends among them. You and your men may have given them a mistaken opinion of me, but *they* have done nothing to become my enemies.

"Second," the captain proceeded, "I have other Indian friends here, the Nez Perces. They are willing to fight, for they have no love of the Blackfeet. But if I throw them into *your* battle, some of them are sure to be killed—needlessly. This fight is none of their quarrel."

Birlock began sneering at all this concern for what he rated as "cussed Injuns." But the captain's next words straightened his lip.

"Lastly, the wanton way you've destroyed beaver in the Blackfoot country and the region bordering it has earned you, Birlock, a good whipping."

"But great snakes, Cap'n—white men hev got to stick together!"

"I didn't mean I'd stand by and watch you all be killed. Pack and mount. Let's see if we can ride away together."

But the trappers' first sign of preparation to leave the

spot spurred the Blackfeet to action. With an outburst of wilder yells, they threw their riders around the entire group of whites and Nez Perces. However, they kept out of effective range of the Hawken rifles.

"I'll signal for a parley with the Blackfeet," Captain Bonneville told Birlock. "I carry a pipe which one of their chiefs gave me as a token of friendship and a safe-passage talisman. If I convince them that my men did *not* trap on Roubideaux's River nor destroy beaver lodges, I am confident they will let *my* party ride away. I think I can get their consent for you to go with us. I shall tell them that you'll give them—as part payment for the mischief you did in their country—all your beaver skins."

"I'll be scalped ef I will!" stormed Birlock.

"You'll be scalped if you don't," said the captain calmly. "I've told you I'll not fight in your unworthy cause. And, short of horses as you are, you can't run away from the Indians and take the fur with you. That was proved when they caught you, here." He rode out of the group, holding his rifle arm's length above his head. Then he leaned from his saddle and laid it on the ground and rode on, unarmed, toward the Blackfeet.

"They kin hev the fur," Birlock called after him.

Captain Bonneville took off his hat to better show that he was the Chief-who-has-been-scalped. Laramie, also unarmed, rode on one side of him. Nat took his usual place on the other. Laramie made the peace sign—the right hand, palm upward, going forward from the heart. Three Blackfoot chiefs met them halfway.

None of these was Big Swan, beside whom they had

fought in the Tetons . . . or Stabs Bear, who had given Captain Bonneville the carved red pipe. One of them, Wandering Spirit, recognized the pipe, however. All of them had heard of the promise of safe-conduct that went with it to Captain Bonneville. But they all believed that the Chief-who-has-been-scalped had broken *his* promise not to molest the beaver.

Patiently, Captain Bonneville repeated to them that *other* white men had been in the valley of Roubideaux's River before him. That it was those men who had broken the beaver lodges. This talk was through Laramie, in the sign language. The chiefs debated whether to believe the captain. At last they told him to take his own men and go.

The captain offered the beaver skins in exchange for permission to take the American Fur Company trappers with him. The Blackfeet replied that, by killing those trappers, they could have the fur anyway—with guns and horses.

To Nat, the tension of this soundless conversation grew tighter and tighter. He could read the replies as the stony-faced Wandering Spirit "threw the sign." He could see the angry restlessness of the warriors back of him and knew that the Blackfeet wanted battle. He knew, also, that the Nez Perces, eager young men, wanted to win honor and to avenge their tribesmen killed last autumn. Birlock and his men were furious at what they considered treachery on the part of Captain Bonneville. Even Fenton and his men thought this a good time to teach the Blackfeet not to bother white men, no matter what they did. Nat couldn't see how the captain could prevent a battle when almost everyone here wanted to fight.

But Captain Bonneville did not give up. He spoke to the chiefs earnestly, vehemently. And though they had to wait for Laramie to silently relay the exact meaning, they understood the sincerity in the captain's tones. They agreed at last.

"Bring the fur," the captain called.

"Come an' git it!" Birlock snarled. "They'll shoot us down as soon as we give away our barricade."

"They'll keep their word—even if you wouldn't," the captain answered. "The fur is worth but little more than the goods you stole from me, so I have a right to bargain with it, especially in a deal to save *your* lives. Fenton, you and your men bring the skins."

For a moment it looked like there would be a fight between the two bands of trappers before Fenton's men could carry out their orders. Nat knew the Blackfeet recognized what a choice time this was to strike at their enemies again.

Perhaps Birlock and his men saw this, too. Sullenly, they gave over the result of their winter's work, to the last pack of skins.

During these slow minutes that were stretched tighter than a bowstring, Nat's eyes swept the ranks of Blackfoot warriors. He was watching for the first lifting of a bow or gun, the first tightening of knees on horses' ribs. For one hot-headed warrior, rebelling against his chiefs, might trip the delicate balance in which the situation hung and sweep forward a renewal of the attack. So evenly matched were

215

the opposing forces that the fight could not end until a great many on each side had been killed.

In spite of Nat's concentration, his moving gaze tripped on something. It caught an instant, and went on, but came back—to a brown horse.

Many horses are brown. This one had no markings. But he had a shape and style, a width of forehead, a way of holding his ears—a *something* about him—that, even at fifty yards, made the boy think of Pierre.

Quickly, Nat lifted his eyes to the rider of the brown horse. Except that the Indian was young, the familiarity he sought disappeared. The way the Indian had braided his hair was the way of the Blackfeet massed around him. It struck Nat as strange that he wore no feathers or ornaments and carried no weapons. His face, painted like the others, was expressionless.

But his hands were moving, cautiously. Suddenly Nat realized that, since no one faced the Blackfeet but himself, Laramie and Captain Bonneville, and the latter two were absorbed in their dealing with the chiefs, those discreet movements were meant for him, Nat. The Indian was "throwing the sign."

Nat read the repeated symbols. The quiver that had run through him when his eyes rested on the brown horse that looked like Pierre almost rocked him now.

"Talks-with-horses, I am Far Eagle." Nat could see it then. It *was* Far Eagle and it *was* Pierre, plain as day!

It took all the self-control the white boy had been a year in learning to keep his gladness from shouting back—to keep his body motionless, his face blank. But only ten feet in front of him were the three Blackfoot chiefs, and behind them, not too far away to see any recognition or reply Nat might try to send, were the ranks of Blackfoot warriors.

Plainly, Far Eagle was a captive. On his way home last fall to the land of the Absaroka he had *not* been able to get through the Blackfoot country. But his courage, his endurance, or some other quality Far Eagle had shown that his captors admired, had overcome their hatred of a Crow. They were doing something not uncommon among the Indians of the northern plains. They were making—or trying to make—him into a warrior of their own tribe.

Now, if Nat revealed that Far Eagle was signaling him, a plot to escape would be suspected. The young Crow would suffer. In this tense moment, it would be a skull-crushing blow of a war club or the thrust of a lance.

In addition, at this critical point in Captain Bonneville's negotiations, the detection of a secret message from his party to anyone in the Indian ranks might be considered double dealing. "Talking with two tongues" was the most contemptible crime in the Indian list. The captain's great and singlehanded effort to arrange a truce would collapse. The war whoop would ring again and arrows and bullets fly—with Far Eagle and Nat on opposite sides!

So, with forced calmness, Nat faced his first and best Indian friend who, for half a year, he had feared might be dead, but who now sat within easy calling distance on the brown horse, Pierre. All that the white boy could do was twist one moccasined foot slowly from side to side in the hope that Far Eagle would see the slight movement and know that he was recognized.

217

CHAPTER 15

Raid

Yes, surely Far Eagle understood, for while the Blackfoot warriors around him still glared at the white men and their Nez Perce allies, the Crow boy continued to move his hands unobserved. His next message in the hand talk was startling, too.

"Blackfeet catch Square-jaw. Square-jaw have the big pinto. Have horse with spotted rump, have white horse, and more. Now Blackfeet have them. But Square-jaw strong like two men. Last night he break thongs. Get cut in neck but kill two guards and get away."

In that message was a lot more for Nat to think about! And for the present to keep wholly to himself, for, though the packs of beaver skins were being handed over, the three chiefs were eagle-eyed as ever. Nat could understand all the better the gunpowder quality of their hatred of white men, since he now knew that Tarno had just killed two of their band.

But Kiowa and the other horses Nat and his companions

218

wanted so greatly were no longer in the hands of just one man. They were in the possession of the Blackfeet!

The chiefs called up braves to carry away the packs of beaver pelts, which were the price of freedom for the American Fur Company trappers. The two parties to the conference made no pledges, smoked no pipe of peace. Warily as ever, they rode back to their respective bands. They picked up their weapons. Nat was bursting to tell the news about Far Eagle and what he had learned of Tarno and their stolen horses, but he knew his party must stay on sharpest alert until the Blackfeet *proved* the fight was over.

Besides, facing the captain was the snarling Birlock crew. Nat felt the air still snapping with tension. He quietly drew an arrow from the quiver on his shoulder and fitted it to the string of his horn bow.

It was a right hunch that made him do it. As Captain Bonneville turned to give an order to Fenton, Nat saw Birlock throw up his rifle. The boy yelled.

But he also made a whiplike draw of his bow and released his arrow.

It struck first, but the rifle roared instantly. No doubt the arrow's piercing blow on Birlock's shoulder jerked his aim, but Captain Bonneville lurched from his saddle.

Instantly, Fenton's men leveled their guns on the group behind Birlock. But none of them raised their guns. Birlock's reckless action drew no support from his crew. By now, he had dropped his rifle. Fenton and Laramie whipped a thong under the big man's elbows and drew them together behind him. Birlock howled in pain as they moved his right arm. The flint head of Nat's arrow was set deep in the bone of his shoulder joint.

Fenton yanked it out without ceremony. Laramie joined Nat, who knelt beside Captain Bonneville.

"Is he dead?" Nat gasped his question, half stunned by the awful possibility. Laramie, with a glance at the wound on the side of the captain's head, placed his hand inside his leader's hunting shirt.

"*Non!*" he cried joyfully. "His heart beats. He is only stunned."

The Blackfeet must have seen all this disturbance among the white men, but took no advantage of it. Keeping their bargain, they began to withdraw. Laramie and Fenton knew their side must do likewise. The limp form of the captain was thrown across Laramie's saddle. The Canadian sat behind it and held his leader in place. The cavalcade moved away and finally a swell in the plain hid the Indians from sight.

It was dusk, and a stream had been found where the men were making camp, before Captain Bonneville recovered consciousness. He was still weak and sick, for the bullet had done more than graze his skull. It had struck a savage, glancing blow. Nat had told Laramie about Far Eagle and all that he had learned from his Crow friend. But they said nothing to the captain, except to tell him that there had been no battle—that so far both sides had kept the agreement that he and the chiefs had made. He ordered a doubling of the night guard.

Nat and Laramie were on the first watch—and at adjoining posts. Soon after dark, Nat sought Laramie but couldn't find him. He waited . . . Laramie returned soon with Ten Owl and another Nez Perce named Towassis—Bowstring. Nat overheard their few words and learned that Bowstring was to take Laramie's place. Nat made his presence known by the shrill call of a prairie owl.

"Big Medicine?" Laramie questioned into the dark.

Nat joined them. "I am going with you," he said firmly.

"Who said anybody goin' anywhere?" evaded Laramie.

"I know that you and Ten Owl are going to steal back our horses," Nat said. "My horse is among them and my best friend is a prisoner of the Blackfeet. Maybe I can get them both."

There was protest against the white boy's going. There would be plenty of danger. But Nat insisted and Laramie really believed that his "medicine" brought luck to any enterprise in which he took part. It wasn't hard to win Laramie's consent.

Ten Owl's respect for the white boy had been won by Nat's skill in the buffalo hunt and his quickness in protecting Captain Bonneville. The young chief disappeared, then returned with another of his warriors, who took Nat's place at standing guard.

The three said nothing to anyone else of their intentions. The whole band of Nez Perces would have been glad to go along and take as many horses from the Blackfeet as they could get. With Ten Owl, though, the main motive seemed to be a matter of tribal pride—to restore to Captain Bonneville the white horse which was a gift from a senior Nez Perce chief.

221

Nat believed honestly that the captain was too ill to be consulted. He was pretty sure, too, that his leader would not approve the risk. But tonight, while the Blackfeet were still within twenty miles of them, was their one chance to recover their horses! And to Nat and Laramie the urge was overpowering.

They had no feelings of wrong about stealing the horses from the Blackfeet, although it was not the Blackfeet who had stolen the horses from them. To Laramie and Nat, the Paloos and Kiowa were still *their* horses—and the Indians had come by them easily enough in taking them from Tarno. The Blackfeet had also taken with the horses, so far as anyone knew, a wealth of beaver skins that were in Tarno's possession and that really belonged to Captain Bonneville. That was fur which had *not* been trapped in Blackfoot country. Part of it had been obtained by Tarno from the Shoshonies, in exchange for the goods he had stolen when he took the horses, 'way out in Oregon.

But in Nat's mind there was one intention that assured him that he was doing right. That purpose was—if any possible opportunity opened—to free Far Eagle.

Nat, Laramie and Ten Owl slipped out to their picketed horses and rode quietly away. They had not hampered themselves with their long, heavy rifles or even with Nat's bow and quiver. They carried knives to cut picket lines and hobbles. And *kopluts*—the short Nez Perce war clubs.

When they were out of hearing of the camp, they put their mounts to a swinging canter. They knew only the general direction taken by the Blackfeet but they headed for a certain creek along which the Indians were likely to

222

have camped. Near midnight, they reached the creek. After following it for a mile or two, Ten Owl lifted his hand for them to stop.

"Smell the camp," he announced.

The still coldness of the night whetted all odors. Even Nat could pick some of them from the blend that hung in the air. There was the smell of moistness. That rose from the creek. There was the smell of quick-growing grass and spearmint from the meadow along the stream. More faintly, there was the smell of horses. Smoke and the odor of roasted meat hung in the air long after the fires had been put out.

The three rode on cautiously and soon many grazing horses could be seen dimly by the starlight.

They left the horses they were riding at quite a distance from the grazing herd, so there would be no whinnying. With increased caution, they went forward, first at a crouching walk, then on hands and knees. Ten Owl chose to follow the edge of the willows that fringed the creek. They were sure that the warriors were sleeping in this shelter, but its shadow was protection to them, also. And it was well to locate the camp, the point of danger, before anything else was tried. This band of Blackfeet was a war party, so there were no women and children with them; therefore no tepees by which the camp could be easily seen. But at least that meant there were no dogs. And how thankful Nat was that there was no moon!

There was danger enough in the fact that the horses would smell the strangers. Even though they did not take

223

alarm, a watchful pause in their grazing might be noticed by the camp guards.

Just in front of them and as though out of the ground itself, one of these guards rose to a keener listening position on one knee. If a short bow had been in his hands, he might have drawn it. But the arm of Ten Owl with his *kopluts* was quicker than the Blackfoot's attempt to raise his gun. There was a soft thud. The sentry slumped to the ground again.

Laramie, with the handle of his war club, quickly pried off the hammer of the guard's fusee.

To Nat's great relief, the young Nez Perce chief did not stab and scalp the Blackfoot, now so completely in his power. He was holding his fierce instincts and thirst for vengeance remarkably in check, to keep the promise made by Captain Bonneville that there would be no more fighting. What he did was gag the Blackfoot and tie him to a willow, for there was no telling how soon the guard might regain consciousness.

The three raiders crept on. They could depend on it that the three horses they wanted would be tied near the camp. The Blackfoot horsemen would appreciate the value of the white, the Paloos and the big pinto enough for that. But the next bend in the edge of the willows revealed a whole line of close-picketed horses, most of them of odd colors or piebald markings. Only Laramie's Paloos, with its spotted rump, was so rare that there was no other that could be confused with it.

Kiowa, Nat distinguished from ten or a dozen pintos,

partly by the stallion's more than average height but mainly by the striking pattern of his markings.

But before they cut loose either of these, they must find White Thunder. He would loom most clearly in the dark. Only—there were *five* all-white horses! The one they wanted was average in size. Ten Owl did not know him well, for the young chief came from a different village from that of Speaking Thunder. For that matter, Nat and Laramie had known the white horse for a period of but twenty days and that time was two months past.

Inch by silent inch, Nat and his companions moved among the horses. The first white one was a mare. The second one had a sagging under lip. The third one they studied for some time before Nat pointed out that the horse was "cow-hocked," that is, he stood with his hocks too close together, which would give him a poor gait when running.

But the last two white horses seemed as alike as two antelope.

"*You* got to pick him," Laramie whispered to Nat. "You took care of him from de Imnaha to Fort Walla Walla. An' it's a horse, I think, must be your *wyakin*."

Nat took the risk of laying hold the rawhide picket line and creeping to the head of the nearest white horse. It sniffed at him . . . and pulled away. Never forgetting stealth, Nat tried the other one. There was the same inquisitive, slightly suspicious sniffing . . . a pause . . . then a low—a fortunately very low—chucking sound of recognition! It was White Thunder. Ten Owl cut the picket line.

"I'll be a minute," whispered Nat.

225

"You be a mighty short one," ordered Laramie. Nat slipped away toward Kiowa.

The pinto knew him, of course. He came several steps toward Nat as soon as he got the scent. The boy quickly pressed the soft nostrils of the stallion as a warning against a nicker. He cut the line and looped it around the pinto's jaw to make an Indian bridle.

Keeping on the side farthest from the camp, Nat rose slowly, caught the mane and leaped to Kiowa's back—or side, rather, so as to make no change in the pinto's outline against the faint light of the sky. He set Kiowa moving very slowly—not back toward Laramie but among the horses along the edge of the camp. Mainly he let the stallion go where he would.

Nat's problem was to keep Kiowa from going too fast— which would attract attention, for the big pinto, as much as Nat let him, moved purposefully until he reached a small brown horse.

Again there was a silent recognition. In spite of Nat's haste and fear of an alarm, the nuzzling of Pierre brought a tightening to his throat. But, absorbed in his greater purpose, he was thinking that Far Eagle must be near. He must have tied Pierre as close as possible to the place where he would sleep—or lie awake, rather, for surely he would be expecting Nat. Oh, surely he would believe that his friend would come and try to free him!

Kiowa had found Pierre for Nat, that was the first step in finding Far Eagle. But now would Pierre nicker and unintentionally betray Nat—and Laramie and Ten Owl—

as the white boy moved away from him? The best N
could do to prevent that was to leave Kiowa with Pierre.

He slipped softly to the ground and crept toward the
willow bushes. It was his first movement during this night
in which he was entirely alone—one boy in the camp of a
hundred warriors! For the first time, Nat's fear, which of
course had been in him all along, almost got out from under
the control of his purpose. It took the greatest struggle so
far in his life to go on—to think only that *now* was his
chance to free Far Eagle.

He breathed deeply, until his heart slowed a little in its
thumping. Then he made the squeak of a meadow mouse.
Keyed tight, he listened. But he heard only the moving
about of the many horses. He crawled a little nearer and
squeaked again. This time he thought his strained ears
caught a repetition.

He gained the deeper shadow along the edge of the
willows, then squeaked a third time in inquiry. The answer
came, startlingly near him. Yet, between him and the
place where he had located the sound, came slow, even
breathing. Nat moved around the shadow of the sleeping
warrior. His eyes, thoroughly accustomed to the darkness,
made out two more forms. One bulked large, under a robe.
The other was slim and uncovered beside it.

Nat's feather-light, exploring fingers were met by the
searching ones of Far Eagle. For a moment their hands
pressed with deep meaning. Then Nat put the hilt of his
knife into the hand of Far Eagle. He waited while the
Indian boy softly cut the thongs that tied his other wrist
to the wrist of the sleeping warrior beside him.

There was no movement, but the sound of that warrior's deep and regular breathing could be heard no longer. The boys knew he was awake.

Almost breathless, they waited through seconds that were long and brittle. It was too much to hope that the warrior would go back to sleep. And Nat knew that Laramie was sure to come in search of him. That would double the danger of rousing the camp.

Nat's fingers tugged, lightly but urgently, on Far Eagle's arm. The Crow boy sighed, freely as one does in sleep, and rolled away from the warrior. But it didn't work. The man sat up like a Jack-in-the-box and reached for Far Eagle.

Desperation steeled Nat's arm. The *kopluts* in his right hand fell.

Again that soft thud and the muffled sound of the stunned warrior dropping back on his buffalo robe. Near them, the forms of many light sleepers came to a sitting posture. Nat, from the crouched position in which he had struck, flattened again to the ground. But a warrior doubled forward at him. The boys sprang up and ran.

"*Howgh-owgh!*" rang the Blackfoot war cry. "*Howgh-owgh!*"

Yet it flashed through Nat's mind, with the speed with which thoughts come in times of danger, that at least that dreaded yell would warn Laramie and Ten Owl. It would mean "every man for himself" and send them speeding away on their fast horses. They need take no more risk on his account.

As he'd never run before, Nat ran toward Kiowa. Even

so, he knew Far Eagle was pulling him. The young Crow, who had been called Runs Ahead because of his speed, made it possible for his friend to reach the pinto far enough ahead of the warriors to throw himself on the stallion's back before he was clutched or stabbed. Far Eagle slashed Pierre's picket line and was on the brown horse in what seemed one movement.

Their horses leaped to full speed. A few arrows swished by the boys. A fusee banged. But Nat and Far Eagle were low on the necks of Kiowa and Pierre, and there was too much confusion behind them for the Indians to risk many shots.

The running, the yelling, had frightened many of the Indian horses. They were hard to mount quickly. The rearing and plunging animals made it perilous for both pursued and pursuers. Tied or hobbled horses were in the way, everywhere. Kiowa and Pierre managed to get through them but more than one warrior's horse somersaulted with him over a picket pin or a stretched picket line. So the boys broke free of the horse herd with a few yards lead and the brown horse and the tall pinto flattened to the dark prairie.

There were more shots and a rising drum of hoofbeats. But off to their left, Nat heard the shrill Nez Perce war cry. That would be Ten Owl. The Nez Perce yells swelled like a chorus, and for a moment Nat thought Ten Owl's entire band had come along, after all. But then he recognized the tones of Laramie in nearly half the racket and he remembered how one coyote can sound like ten. *Itsi-yiyi*, he knew, was not the only clever fellow.

229

Trail of the Pinto to Oregon

But the yells had an effect on the Blackfeet, for many of them swung off to surround their horse herd. There, truly enough, Ten Owl and Laramie were starting a stampede.

However, plenty of the Blackfeet still rode hotly behind Nat and Far Eagle. An arrow stung as it brushed Nat's thigh. Bent close to Kiowa's neck, he was a small target. The fear that clutched now was that Kiowa would be hit —or Far Eagle—or Pierre.

But they raced on. And through Nat's fear surged up a tingling elation. He didn't think about it. He didn't have to think to know that it came to him from the powerful horse under him, running zestfully in the dark—from Kiowa, *his* Kiowa, at last!

For, barring a fall from a prairie-dog hole, Nat was confident no horse could catch him. About Laramie and Ten Owl, with their splendid horses, he had little worry, either. His concern now was for Far Eagle. Maybe the Blackfeet weren't gaining on Pierre, but the brown horse wasn't keeping up with Kiowa, so Nat swung back. He circled behind Pierre and brought Kiowa up close to his flank.

"Come!" he shouted to Far Eagle.

The Crow boy knew his meaning and grabbed Nat's waist. Without a break in the stride of either horse he swung over behind his friend on the pinto. Maybe Pierre, unburdened, could keep up. Earnestly, Nat hoped so. But Kiowa, doubled loaded, had once before run away from the Blackfeet.

They sped on, and gradually the drum of pursuing hoofs

230

dimmed . . . finally died out, except the steady beat of the hoofs of Pierre. Nat reined in. Listening intently, the two boys could hear only the thin wail of a far-off coyote. It had a triumphant, derisive note. Ten Owl, probably, was signaling Nat that he and Laramie were safe—or laughing at the Blackfeet—or both.

It took a while to realize it fully—that at last Nat and Far Eagle, Kiowa and Pierre were together. The boys leaped down, and while the horses got their wind, Nat and Far Eagle gripped each other's shoulders and whirled in a celebration dance.

← ← ← CHAPTER **16**

Cache

The two young friends rode on in the direction in which Nat believed Captain Bonneville's camp lay. And of course the boys talked. Nat found that he had forgotten very little of the Crow language, nor did he often get it mixed with the Nez Perce.

"How soon after you left us were you captured by the Blackfeet?" was one of the questions Nat asked.

"Not till the brown horse and I were nearly home," Far Eagle answered. "We were through the Tetons. Pierre was so nearly starved and I was so nearly frozen that we were stupid. In a storm, we stumbled into an Indian camp. The snow was so deep and we were so worn out that, when I saw that the Indians were Blackfeet, I knew it was no use to try to run from them. Instead, I asked them for food."

"What did they do to you?"

"Some of them were very angry when they saw I am an Absaroka. They tied me to a tree and said, at least, that they would kill me by ways that take a long time. They

CACHE

thought they would make me beg or cry. I did not. . . .
But a few of the warriors had been with Big Swan in the
battle in the Tetons. They saw Pierre was your horse.
Then they remembered me as your prisoner. They had
promised at that time that they would not kill me, so they
would not make liars of themselves by killing me now.
That, I think, is what they must have said among themselves. They cut me free and fed me. They have taught
me to speak their Siksiki language and have told me many
times what cowards the Absaroka are and how brave are
the Siksiki." Far Eagle gave a short laugh. "They thought
they were making me into a Blackfoot!"

"Did you never try to escape?" Nat asked.

"Once, after my leg was well. But I did not get far.
For that they tied my hands together behind my back and
tied a long cord to my wrists. With the cord over my
shoulder, they led me by it behind a horse for a day. I
knew that if I stumbled or if the rider struck his horse,
both my arms would be jerked out of joint at the shoulders."

"And you kept up with the horse!"

"I still have my arms," Far Eagle answered. "You can
do what you have to. It is you, Talks-with-horses, who have
done the hard thing in getting me free. I will never forget.
What have you seen since I started for the country of the
Absaroka?"

Nat told briefly of his stay with the Nez Perces—the
Apupé, to Far Eagle. The good he had to say of them was
not disputed. The Crows and the *Apupé*, though living

233

far apart, were friends. He told of the making of the horn bow and of Hin-mot and the wolverine.

Nat also told of his canoe voyage and of Fort Vancouver. But particularly he related the treachery of Tarno. He asked Far Eagle one question that had puzzled him.

"How did the Blackfeet catch Square-jaw when he had Kiowa—and the other very fast horses?"

"In the night," replied Far Eagle, "Square-jaw rode away from the camp of those other trappers who are not of the Chief-who-has-been-scalped. The Blackfeet were watching the camp, planning an attack. Square-jaw rode into a group of them in a thicket of trees. Your big horse, which he was riding, smelled Indians and tried to turn, but he struck it with the butt of his gun. Then the Blackfeet seized him and his rifle before he could fire a shot."

"Square-jaw had many packs of beaver skins," Nat said. "The Blackfeet got them, didn't they?"

Far Eagle's answer surprised him. "No, he had seven horses but they carried only one pack of skins."

"Then what did he do with those thirteen hundred plew?" Nat demanded, mostly of himself. Far Eagle gave only an inquiring cluck. So the white boy explained how Tarno, though all the past year in the employ of the American Fur Company, had not delivered the stolen fur to Birlock. And now Nat knew he had not brought it near to Birlock's camp.

"He hid the beaver." Far Eagle supplied the natural answer.

"And that was why he killed the Shoshoni that was with

CACHE

him!" Nat exclaimed. "So no one but himself would know
where they had made the cache. I wonder . . ."

"Yes?" inquired Far Eagle.

"Those empty caches of the captain's. They're not a
great distance away. What could be more handy for him?"

Further words were not necessary for the two boys to
turn their horses in the direction of the caches.

They had not forgotten the Blackfeet. They listened
frequently but their sharp ears could hear no sound, so
they did not push their horses faster than a steady canter.
They reasoned that the Blackfeet, when they took stock
of their losses, had not so much reason to be furious.
Two of their warriors, no doubt, had memorable head-
aches. They had lost a Crow captive and five captured
horses, counting the one on which Tarno had escaped. They
were still ahead by three horses taken from Tarno and the
three which Nat, Laramie and Ten Owl had left near their
camp. And they had the pack of beaver skins, worth twenty
horses, which Tarno had taken from Birlock's camp.
They should call tonight's deal quits.

But you couldn't tell. The Blackfeet were a haughty
people and might go a long way to avenge the insult of any
sort of raid on their camp.

The new direction of Nat and Far Eagle took them past
the place where the Shoshonies had buried their comrade.
Nat had not expected to be able to recognize the spot, but
he was shocked by the way he was able to do so. Their
horses shied at an open hole. The grave was empty!

The two boys rode on. Soon dawn began to break above
the eastern mountains; first as a paling of the inky sky,

235

then as a spreading tinge of yellow and green, deepening and changing to gold and rose. A hundred little horned larks, unseen around them, started to sing that it was day —and spring. Before sunrise, the boys could hear the booming of sage cocks and even see them at times, ruffled out of all resemblance to birds, as they strutted their strange mating dance.

The sun hit the top of the butte where yesterday, when approaching from the other direction, Ten Owl had seen the shadow of the hidden warrior. Now a warrior stood in full view on the butte's highest point. His arms were stretched wide. The sun burnished them and his bare shoulders and chest.

"He is praying," Far Eagle said respectfully.

The boys believed they were seen and were well aware that they were unarmed. But they did not believe the warrior was an enemy. It might be a Nez Perce looking for Ten Owl, Nat and Laramie. They rode to the butte and around it. They found nothing but the tracks of the horses of the Nez Perces who had encircled it yesterday and the Shoshonies they had found behind it—except for the tracks of one horse that had, with great difficulty, scrambled up its steep, rocky slope.

Then the warrior they had seen appeared again. He was making the peace sign. Nat recognized him as one of the Shoshonies, the youngest and considerably the smallest of the five.

Nat returned the peace sign and signaled the warrior to come down. The Shoshoni did so, on foot. "Where is your horse?" Nat asked—rather clumsily with his hands. He

236

could not yet "speak" the hand talk as well as he could understand it. But he knew no Shoshoni at all.

The man gestured toward the butte top. Then his hands moved so swiftly Nat got lost and had to look to Far Eagle to interpret the signs.

"I have dug up my brother and buried him again," Far Eagle repeated the meaning in Crow. "Up there, where I could leave my horse with him and yet not mark the place to be found by enemies."

"But the horse will starve—" Nat broke out in protest. Then he understood. The Shoshoni meant he had killed the horse on the grave. Only by so doing, he believed, could he save his friend from the tragedy of being afoot in the Spirit Land.

Perhaps the dead warrior *was* this man's blood brother, Nat thought. Of the five Shoshonies, only he had returned to perform this last service for the one Tarno had killed. Now the man was afoot himself and many miles from anywhere. Nat motioned him to get up behind him on Kiowa. In the sign language, Far Eagle explained their purpose of looking for the stolen fur and the Shoshoni nodded his willingness to go with them. His eyes smoldered at the mention of Square-jaw.

As they neared the Snake River, the prairie grew broken and cut by ravines in which brush or timber grew. Nat knew they were nearing the caches. As he was the only one of the three who had ever been to the place, it was up to him now to locate it, for if Tarno, as Nat believed, had used either of the ready-made pits, he would undoubtedly have covered and concealed both. So Nat was studying every hill and knoll, every ravine and grassy flat—and thinking that to go straight to the spot would prove to these two Indians what a skilful Indian *he* had become.

Two crows, cawing loudly, lifted into the air from a pine under which they rode. Such an announcement of their coming was bad, no matter where they were going. Far Eagle checked Pierre, as though to drop back and wait—or make a detour. But Nat, intent on locating the caches, rode on. Far Eagle came up with him, frowning anxiously. Nat's mistake in ignoring caution came near to being his last.

Ahead of them, a gun blazed.

Chips of bark flew into Nat's face from a tree trunk in front and just a little to one side of him. The ricocheting bullet nipped his shoulder and went on with a shrill snarl. Thirty paces ahead of them, the spectre of a shaggy, hatless man, with a blood-blackened rag around his throat, dropped from sight behind a gully bank. *Tarno!* He would be reloading of course.

Surprise had struck Nat like a club. It was doubled by the shock of realizing that they were unarmed. His flinch from the spot where the bullet had struck so near him and the sting of the bark against his face made him throw up a warding arm and sway a little on his horse. Far Eagle spurred toward him, thinking his friend was hurt.

The Shoshoni had thrown himself to the ground from behind Nat as though he *had* been hit.

For an instant the boys scarcely remembered he was with them. Then the Shoshoni reminded them forcefully—by lightly striking Kiowa and Pierre across their noses with his bow. He was turning them—and hitting them on the necks to keep them turning. Nat and Far Eagle stared at him.

Wordlessly and with a slash of his hand across his own mouth to command the boys to silence, he was eloquently motioning them to wheel their horses and run. He gave them no choice. He cut the horses across their rumps with stinging blows. Their hoofs thudded from the spot. Angry amazement flamed in Nat, but before he had checked Kiowa, a gleam of understanding came.

The Shoshoni knew what he was doing. He was counting on it that Square-jaw hadn't seen him, a rather small Indian seated behind Nat. No one expected any horse to be carrying double. Now, as Tarno reloaded his rifle in the shelter of the bank, he would hear the hoofs of both horses galloping off. He would think *all* persons who had approached were running away. He might rise quickly and unguardedly to shoot after them.

Nat and Far Eagle pressed low to their horses' necks but they looked back together—and *did* see Tarno heave himself up with a strangely clumsy motion. There seemed to be a wildness on his face, with his matted hair and beard, that was unnatural, even for the roughest of the mountain men.

He raised his rifle quickly. The boys were still in fair range. Surely once was all that a certain shot like Square-jaw would miss.

Nat expected the rifle's crack, but he heard no sound. He saw the gun drop . . . saw Tarno stagger, then lurch forward. Both of Square-jaw's hands were clutching at the arrow that the Shoshoni, crouching near, had driven through his chest.

When Nat and Far Eagle reached him, he was stone dead.

They found that, when Tarno had escaped from the Blackfeet, he had been shot in the leg as well as stabbed in the neck. A forked stick that had served him as a crutch lay near.

"He must have lost balance on his one good leg, and that was why he missed me," Nat said.

There was a trickle of water in the gully. In the shade of a bush lay part of a deer. The horse on which the man had escaped from the Blackfeet was picketed in a hidden meadow not far away. This was the camp from which Square-jaw, bullheaded as ever, had determined to guard his hidden wealth until he recovered from his wounds and regained, in some way, enough horses to pack two thousand pounds of skins.

The cache needed to be guarded because both Captain Bonneville and Birlock knew its location and might come to the same conclusion that Nat had reached. But when he hid the beaver there, Tarno had expected to use the cache for only a day or two and to be well on the way to St. Louis with the fur by the time either Birlock or the captain guessed it was he who had taken the skins.

At least that was the way Nat figured it out. And then he was struck by another problem. "Were did Square-jaw get a rifle?" he asked, perplexed. "And powder and ball and a knife? He couldn't have picked up all those things while he was escaping from the Blackfeet!"

This puzzled the three of them until the Shoshoni supplied an answer. By examining the gun, powder horn, bullet pouch and knife, he identified all of them as belonging to his dead brother.

"Tarno cached 'em after he shot the Indian," Nat said. "But I bet he never guessed he'd need 'em so soon!"

The Shoshoni picked up the rifle and mounted Tarno's horse. Nat expected him to go with Far Eagle and himself to the camp of Captain Bonneville, but he signed that he no longer wished to go to the rendezvous. He was going home, which meant many "sleeps" down the Snake River, alone. Nat sympathized with him in his sorrow and felt deeply indebted to him. Still, there was nothing he and Far Eagle could do but make the sign of farewell and watch him ride away.

The two boys found the cache. Nat was able to remember its location within a dozen yards. But it was Far Eagle who detected the not-quite-natural spot in the sod. They opened it—enough to make sure the fur was there—then re-covered it, mounted and rode at a distance-eating pace for Captain Bonneville's camp.

Long before they reached it, they saw scattered riders on the horizon. These proved to be Laramie and some of the Nez Perces, hunting for Nat. The scouts recognized Kiowa at a great distance and Laramie's Paloos led the rest of them like an arrow. Smiles and grimaces crossed the Canadian's face, the way the spring sunlight and wind-driven cloud shadows were crossing the land. He brought the Paloos to a stop in a scuff of dust.

"*Sacre bleu*, but I'm glad to find you! Glad for you—

glad for me. De cap'n, I think, goin' skin me for goin' on de raid last night. 'Specially for lettin' *you* go. 'Nat's a *boy*,' he says. 'Can't blame him. But you, Laramie, 'sposed to be growed-up man! 'Sposed to have sense!' Me, I think he goin' to chew up his huntin' knife an' spit it at me! He's about to start out to find de Blackfeet an' bargain for your release. But you *get away*, by gosh! An' you get Far Eagle an' Kiowa an' Pierre, too! Now, I'll tell cap'n eef Nat's a boy—Laramie, he's still in papoose sling!"

Surprisingly, Laramie still had breath.

"We've got news for him," Nat said, meaningfully.

They rode on. Soon Nat told his news to Captain Bonneville.

"*You* are the best news!" the captain said. "Sure, the recovery of thirteen hundred beaver skins puts a very different financial face on my year's work. But that is nothing compared to your safety. I am glad, too, and proud that you secured Far Eagle's release.

"Still," he said, bringing a sternness into his tone with an effort, "you were as undisciplined as a mountain man to go on that raid without permission. I should punish you. But how can I when only yesterday your quickness saved my life?"

The captain moved camp that afternoon, to the Snake River, at a spot near the cache. Birlock and his men had already been permitted to go their empty-handed way toward the rendezvous on the Siskadee Agie—the Green River. Fenton's men buried the body of Tarno, and Captain Bonneville read by the grave the Christian burial service.

242

"That's somethin'," Nat heard one of the trappers remark, "which don't happen to one in a hundred mountain men—even *good* ones!"

Evening came, with the rose and smoky orange of the western sky reflected in the river—this very long river whose water, beyond a hundred canyons, made up a great part of the River of the West, which Nat had voyaged almost to the sea. The twilight faded and the red of campfires danced on the gliding black water, between the clear white light of stars.

The Nez Perces had killed buffalo while on the way to the river. There was the usual roasting of hump-ribs and sirloins, but no hilarity. All were conscious of the possibility of a counterraid by the Blackfeet. But danger was an everyday and everynight thing. It was the fact that the band would divide tomorrow that sobered everyone.

Captain Bonneville had announced his decision to send all the fur now in his possession to St. Louis the quickest way possible, which was by river route—down the Bighorn, the Yellowstone and the Missouri. With the Nez Perces and some of his trappers, the captain would start at once for the rendezvous, where another consignment of trade goods was due to arrive for him by pack train. Fenton and a few of the most reliable trappers would take the fur. Laramie, as the most experienced riverman, would be the guide for the voyage.

"Can I go part way with Laramie?" Nat asked.

"Why do you say 'part way?'" the captain questioned.

"Because the Bighorn River, where he is going, is in the Absaroka country. Far Eagle will want to travel with

Laramie till he finds the village that is his home. That's what I want to do, too, and spend the summer with Far Eagle among the Crows."

The captain smiled, as though humoring a joke. "When would I see you again?" he asked.

"In the early fall," Nat answered earnestly. "There will surely be some bands of the Crows hunting down toward the Siskadee Agie. I'll go with them, and there I'll find you before you start your winter's trapping. And I'll bring you your horses that the men are taking to pack the fur to the Bighorn River."

Captain Bonneville looked at the boy in a new manner. "I believe you mean it," he said.

"Of *course* I mean it! I left Brent Logan when he wanted me to stay in Oregon and came back for this—to find Far Eagle and spend a summer with him."

Far Eagle spoke, slowly. Nat had long believed the young Crow understood what was said around him but these were the first words of English anyone had heard him use.

"Let Talks-with-horses come. My lodge is his lodge. My robe and my food bowl, they are his. His horses and your horses will be safe and all my people will be glad that he is there."

"We-ll," yielded the captain, "it does seem, Nat, that you can take care of yourself."

"You bet my life he can!" said Laramie. "Him or his *wyakin*."

By now Nat and Far Eagle were two tired, heavy-eyed, boys. But before they turned in they made the rounds of their horses. Nat had, of course, introduced Far Eagle to

244

Whitefoot and told him of swimming the Snake River. Far Eagle had helped Nat lace a buffalo hide boot on the split hoof of Kosooyeen. They hobnobbed a while with Pierre, and also with Kiowa. Then they stumbled toward their buffalo robes.

"Talks-with-horses, I must give you a new name," said Far Eagle. "I shall call you Many Horses."

"You can't have too many good ones," said Nat as he rolled up in the soft fur. "It's queer about that, too," he added. He was at that place on the way to sleep where whatever it was he wanted to say seemed *very* important, though he couldn't remember why.

"Queer about what?" came, muffled, from Far Eagle.

"About owning the best horse in the world—Kiowa. It doesn't make a fellow think any less of the . . ."

He didn't quite make it. Far Eagle wouldn't have heard him, anyway.

J. PAUL LOOMIS

says of his life and interests, "In my early years I lived in Alaska, then Kansas, then Saskatchewan. In each place, all the hours possible were spent in the woods, on creek banks, on the lakes— or on a horse. However, enough of this outdoor life was sacrificed in begrudged fragments for me to complete a course at Kansas State College. Next there was service in the Canadian Army, part of it in Siberia. To reclaim some of this lost time, my wife Julie and I took, as a honeymoon, a two-month canoe trip through the Rocky Mountains. One can do that on the Upper Peace River; nowhere else.

"Twelve years of Canadian ranching gave us much worth remembering; the drum of hoofs on sod while riding home in the mystic dawn from a barn dance, blazing mountainsides of autumn color, the endless squeal of sleigh runners on a fifty-mile trip to the nearest hospital at forty below, the relief of seeing ribby cattle eating grass after a winter that was six—instead of the usual five —months long.

"We don't live in the past; it's dead. But our love of the outdoors, of horses, hiking, bird study—our interest in Indians, true people of the outdoors—continues very much alive. We still have our canoe, using it on the ocean at Santa Barbara, where we live, though a canoe in California is as untraditional as a pack burro in Maine.

"These outdoor interests have moved us from coast to mountains to many parts of Mojave Desert to coast again; to Hawaii, back to Alaska twice. They show in our four children, too. I build houses now for other people—we're planning a new one for ourselves in the mountains overlooking the Santa Barbara Channel— but in the many years that I've scribbled on all my margins of time I can't recall *writing* of anything that took place under a roof."